THE
FORCED BRIDE
OF ALAZAR

BY
KATE HEWITT

First Published in Great Britain 2017
By Mills & Boon, an imprint of HarperCollins*Publishers*
1 London Bridge Street, London, SE1 9GF

© 2017 Kate Hewitt

ISBN: 978-0-263-06886-3

Printed and bound in Great Britain
by CPI Antony Rowe, Chippenham, Wiltshire

After spending three years as a die-hard New Yorker, **Kate Hewitt** now lives in a small village in the English Lake District with her husband, their five children and a golden retriever. In addition to writing intensely emotional stories she loves reading, baking, and playing chess with her son—she has yet to win against him, but she continues to try. Learn more about Kate at kate-hewitt.com.

Books by Kate Hewitt

Mills & Boon Modern Romance

Moretti's Marriage Command
Inherited by Ferranti
Kholodov's Last Mistress

Seduced by a Sheikh

The Secret Heir of Alazar

The Billionaire's Legacy

A Di Sione for the Greek's Pleasure

Secret Heirs of Billionaires

Demetriou Demands His Child

One Night With Consequences

Larenzo's Christmas Baby

The Marakaios Brides

The Marakaios Marriage
The Marakaios Baby

Rivals to the Crown of Kadar

Captured by the Sheikh
Commanded by the Sheikh

Visit the Author Profile page
at millsandboon.co.uk for more titles.

To Jenna, thanks for all your encouragement
and chats-by-text.
See you in Orlando?!
Love, K.

CHAPTER ONE

'I HAVE GOOD NEWS, *habibti.*'

Johara Behwar gazed in surprise at her father striding towards her. She was standing in the garden of the family villa in Provence, the dusty-sweet smell of lavender scenting the air, the sun shining benevolently down on a world on the cusp of summer. Her father's visits to their villa in France were precious and rare, and he'd only been there last week. To see him again was indeed unexpected. 'Good news—' She almost said *again* but then she thought better of it. Her father had not viewed the end of her engagement last week in the same shining light that she had.

'Yes, I think you will be very pleased,' Arif continued. 'And I, of course, am pleased when you are pleased.' He walked towards her, a smile creasing his weathered face, his hands outstretched. Johara smiled back, caught up in his cheerful mood.

'I'm pleased simply to see you, Father. That alone is a treat.'

'You are so kind, *habibti*. And in return here is a treat for you.' He took a small velvet pouch from his breast pocket and handed it to Johara.

She drew a diamond pendant from within the blue velvet, the jewels winking in the bright sunlight. 'It's lovely. Thank you, Father.' Obediently, because she knew her father expected it, she clasped it around her neck, the heart shape encrusted with diamonds nestling in the hollow of her throat. It was indeed lovely, but, considering how quiet her life was, she had little need or place to wear it. Still, she appreciated the thought he'd given.

'What is this good news?' she asked as Arif took hold of her hands.

'I have renegotiated your marriage.' Arif squeezed her hands as his smile widened, triumph glinting in his eyes. Johara stared at her father, confusion making her mind spin even as sudden dread seeped like acid into her stomach. The diamond pendant felt cold against her skin. This was not the good news he'd said it was. This wasn't good news at all.

'Renegotiated?' she repeated faintly. Her hands felt icy encased in her father's. 'But you told me barely a week ago that Malik—I mean His Highness—had ended our engagement.' She'd had six days first for that news to sink in—and then to revel in the glorious freedom she'd never thought to possess. The marriage she'd been trying not to think about and dreading at the same time would no longer happen. She'd felt as if the shackles she hadn't realised she'd been wearing had suddenly fallen off, leaving her feeling light, as if she could fly. She was *free*—free to do as she liked, and in a heady moment she'd let herself think about an independent future, maybe even going to university. The whole world had beckoned, shining and wide open for the first time in her life.

And now... 'How can it be renegotiated? You told me that His Highness was...was infertile.' It seemed indelicate to mention such a thing, but her father had not spared her the details last week, when he'd flown to France to inform her that Malik al Bahjat, heir to the Sultanate of Alazar, had called off their wedding. He'd been furious on her behalf, storming and stomping around, and he had ignored Johara's stammering attempts to placate him and explain that she really didn't mind not getting married to Malik, or, in fact, not getting married at all. She hadn't quite dared to tell her father that she preferred it. After a lifetime of being reminded where her duty lay that seemed a step too far, even as she'd told herself her father surely only wanted her happiness.

'Yes, yes,' Arif said now with a touch of impatience. 'But Malik is no longer the heir, and we thank heaven that you did not marry him before this happened. *That* would have been a disaster.'

Johara agreed, but she doubted it was for the same reason as her father. A week of freedom had made her realise how unwelcome an arranged marriage was. Malik was a virtual stranger and a life bound in duty had lost any lustre it might have possessed. But she knew her father would not agree. So what was going on? If not Malik, then…?

Arif dropped her hands to rub his own together in obvious satisfaction. 'It has all worked out so well for us, Jojo,' he said, using the childhood nickname she hadn't heard in years. 'For you.'

An instant and instinctive disagreement was on the tip of her tongue, but Johara swallowed it down. She never disagreed with her father. She hated to see the smile fade from her father's face, the shadows of disappointment enter his eyes.

Invoking her father's displeasure always felt like the sun disappearing behind a cloud, a sudden chill entering the air and her heart. Her mother's love had long since gone, and taking away her father's attention was a further blow she knew she could not withstand. 'Tell me what has happened, please,' she said instead, trying to inject a note of interest in her voice that she was far from feeling.

'Azim has returned!' Arif spoke with a joy Johara didn't understand. The name was familiar, and yet...

'Azim...?'

'The true heir of Alazar. He has returned from the dead, or so we all thought him.' Arif shook his head in happy disbelief. 'Truly it is a miracle.'

Azim.' Of course, Azim al Bahjat, Malik's older brother. Stupidly she had not made the association. Azim had been kidnapped twenty years ago, when Johara had only been two. There never had been a ransom note delivered or a body found, and so Azim had remained missing, presumed dead, for two decades. Malik had become the heir, had been the only heir in Johara's mind. Until now.

'Azim,' she said again, the name sounding strange on her tongue. 'What...what happened? How has he returned?'

'He had amnesia, apparently, after the kidnapping. He's been living in Italy for twenty years, not knowing who he was. But then he saw a mention of Alazar on the news and it all came flooding back. He has returned to claim his throne.'

'But...' A realisation was growing in her mind like a sandstorm kicking up in the desert, obliterating rational thought just as the sand blotted out the sky. Surely her father wouldn't...to a complete stranger... 'But what does that have to do with me?' She was afraid she knew the answer.

Arif's smile hardened at the edges. Johara knew that look. She quailed at that look.

'Surely you have guessed, Jojo,' he said, his voice jovial yet with a warning hint of underlying iron. 'Azim is to be your husband.'

Johara's stomach swooped. 'But...but I have never even met him,' she protested, her voice faltering.

'He is the heir.' Arif spoke as if it were obvious. 'Since birth you have been pledged to the heir to the Sultanate. In fact you were meant for Azim before you were betrothed to Malik.'

Shock rippled through her in icy waves. *Meant for Azim.* 'I didn't know that. No one ever said.'

Arif shrugged. 'Why would you know it? He disappeared when you were but a child. But now he has returned, and he shall claim you as his bride.'

It would have seemed romantic in a story or film, the kind of sweeping, fairy-tale gesture, a knight riding on his white steed, to make a girlish heart flutter. Johara's heart felt as if it were made of lead, weighing her down. She didn't want to be *claimed*, and certainly not by this stranger. Not when she'd had the whole world open to her moments ago, when she'd felt free for the first time in her life, able to make her own choices, live her own life.

'This seems rather sudden,' she said, trying not to sound quite as horrified as she felt, because she knew that would displease her father. 'My engagement to Malik al Bahjat only ended a week ago. Perhaps we should wait a little.'

Her father shook his head. 'Wait? Azim is determined to secure his throne, and that includes marriage as soon as possible. In fact he expects you in Alazar by tomorrow afternoon.'

Johara gazed at her father's face, the fixed smile, his bushy eyebrows drawn together, and felt her spirits start a precipitous descent. She'd known where her duty lay as long as she could remember. She'd been told it again and again, reminded that she had been given so much, and this was the way—the only way—she could repay her family.

And she'd *wanted* to repay it, had longed to please the father she rarely saw. She'd been prepared to marry Malik, even if hadn't quite felt real. She'd met him only twice, and spent only a handful of days in Alazar. And then for one brief and tantalising week, she'd imagined a different kind of life. One with choice and opportunity and freedom, where she could pursue her interests, dare to nurture her dreams.

Now, looking at her father's stern face, she realised how foolish and naïve she'd been. Her father was never going to let his only daughter go unmarried. He was a traditional man from a traditional country, and he would see her wed…this time to a man she'd never so much as laid eyes on. A man she knew nothing about, that *no one* knew anything about, because he'd been gone for twenty years.

'Johara?' Arif's voice had turned sharp. 'This is not unwelcome, I trust?'

Johara gazed helplessly at the father she'd always adored. She'd lived a sheltered life, educated at home, her pursuits solitary save for some charitable works her father approved of. Her mother had been distant for years, beset by illness and unhappiness, and so it had been her father's love, his sudden smile, his indulgent chuckle, that she had craved. She could not refuse him this even if she had the opportunity to do so, which she knew she did not.

'No, Father,' she whispered. 'Of course not.'

Azim al Bahjat watched from a window as the sedan with blacked-out windows came up the curving drive of Alazar's palace. The car contained his bride. He had not seen a picture of Johara Behwar, had told himself her looks were irrelevant. She was the intended bride of the future Sultan; the people of Alazar expected him to marry her. Any other choice would be less than second best, and therefore impossible. Nothing would prevent him from securing his inheritance and destiny, from proving himself to the people who had more than half forgotten that he was the real heir, the true Sultan.

A servant rushed forward to open the car door, and Azim leaned closer, curious in spite of himself for this first glimpse of his future bride, the next Sultana of Alazar. He saw a slippered foot first, small and dainty, and then a slim, golden ankle emerging from underneath traditional embroidered robes. Then the whole form appeared, willowy and enticing even beneath the shapeless garment, hair as dark as ink peeking from beneath a brightly coloured hijab.

Johara Behwar tilted her head to gaze up at the palace, and from the window Azim could see her whole face, and appreciate its striking beauty. Large, clear grey eyes framed by sooty lashes and gently arched brows. A pert nose, delicate cheekbones and full, pouty, kissable lips. He registered it only for an instant, for the delectable symmetry of her face was marred by its expression. *Revulsion.* Her eyes were wide and shadowed with it, her mouth thinning to a puckered line of distaste. As she gazed at the palace, a shudder went through her, her shoulders jerking, and for a second she wrapped her arms around herself, as if she needed to hold herself together in order to endure what was to come. *Him.* Then she straightened, steel entering her spine, and started towards the palace like a condemned woman ascending to the gallows.

Quickly Azim stepped away from the window. His stomach clenched and pain stabbed his head in two lightning-like slices. He pressed his fingers to his temples and tried to will it away even though he knew from far too much experience what a pointless exercise that was. So Johara Behwar was disgusted by the prospect of marrying him. It was not really a surprise, and yet...

No, he could not think like that. He had no use for sentiment of any kind, the naïve, youthful longings for some sort of connection with the woman who would be his Sultana. He'd made sure to live his life independently, needing no one. Being dependent on someone, much less actually *caring*, led to weakness and vulnerability. Shame and pain. He knew it too well and he had no intention of courting those awful emotions again.

This was a marriage of convenience and expediency, to secure an alliance and produce an heir. Nothing else mattered. Nothing at all.

Taking a deep breath, Azim dropped his hands from his temples and turned to face the door—and to greet his bride.

Each step down the marble corridor felt like a step towards her doom. Johara told herself she was being fanciful, it couldn't possibly be that bad, but her body disagreed. Nausea churned in her stomach and with a sudden lurch of alarm she turned to the attendant who was escorting her to meet His Royal Highness Azim al Bahjat. 'I think I'm going to be sick.'

The attendant backed away from her as if she'd already thrown up onto his shoes.

'Sick—'

She took a deep breath, doing her best to stay her stomach. She could not lose her breakfast moments before meeting her intended husband. Icy sweat prickled on her forehead and her palms were slick. She felt light-headed, as if the world around her were moving closer and then farther away. Another deep breath. She could do this. She had to do this.

She'd done it before, after all, although she'd been a child when she'd first met Malik, and hadn't realised the import of what was happening. The subsequent few meetings had been brief and businesslike, and Johara had managed not to actually think about what they were discussing, and its lifelong consequences, a wilful ignorance that in hindsight seemed both childish and foolish.

Now she couldn't keep from thinking of them. Azim was an utter stranger, and she'd been passed from one brother to the next like some sort of human parcel. The thought made her stomach churn again.

She'd spent the eight-hour flight from Nice telling herself that she and Azim could, perhaps, come to an amenable agreement. An arrangement, which was what all convenient marriages were. She would present him with a proposal, a sensible suggestion to live mainly separate lives that would, she hoped, be to both of their advantage. If she'd had the foresight and presence of mind, she would have done the same with Malik when they'd first discussed their engagement several years ago. Or perhaps she wouldn't have…it was only since she'd tasted freedom that she'd acquired a desperate appetite for it.

'Are you well, Sadiyyah Behwar?' the attendant asked, all solicitude now that he'd ascertained she wasn't really going to vomit.

Johara lifted her chin and forced a smile. 'Yes, thank you. Please lead on.'

She followed the man down the hallway, her trailing robes whispering against the slick marble floor. Her father had insisted she wear traditional formal dress for the first meeting with Azim, although she had never stood on such ceremony with Malik. She found the garment, with its intricately embroidered and jewelled hem and cuffs, stiff, heavy and uncomfortable, the unfamiliar hijab hot on her head. One more element of this whole affair that felt alien and unwelcome.

The attendant paused before a set of double doors that looked as if they were made of solid gold. Johara had been in the palace a few times before, for her brief meetings with Malik, but they'd always taken place in a small, comfortable room. Azim had chosen far more opulent surroundings for this initial introduction.

'His Highness, Azim al Bahjat,' the attendant intoned, and, with fear coating her insides with ice, Johara stepped into the room.

Sunlight poured from several arched windows, nearly blinding her so she had to blink several times before she caught sight of the man she was meant to marry. He stood in the centre of the room, his body erect and still, his face grave and unsmiling. Even from across the room Johara could see how black and opaque his eyes were, like a starless night in the desert. His dark hair was cut so close she could see the powerful bones of his skull, and a scar snaked from the corner of his left eye to the curve of his mouth, clearly long since healed over although the wounded flesh still looked red and livid. He wore an embroidered linen thobe, the material emphasising his lean, muscular form, broad shoulders tapering to narrow hips and long, powerful legs.

The whole effect was beyond intimidating. Terrifying was the word that came to mind, and she had to fight not to take an instinctive step back towards the doors, towards safety, away from this man whose face even in repose looked frightening. Looked cruel, although perhaps that was simply the darkness of his eyes, the livid red of the scar.

If she looked at his features reasonably, Johara told herself, fighting off the panic, she could see that he was an attractive man, his features even, his nose a straight slash, his mouth a mobile, sensual curve. Underneath his linen thobe his body was powerful and he moved with a graceful fluidity, taking a few steps towards her before stopping to survey her as she was surveying him, those dark eyes sweeping from the crown of her head to the soles of her feet, giving away nothing of what he felt or thought.

Then Azim inclined his head in what Johara supposed was a greeting. His voice, when he spoke, was clipped, cold. 'We will marry in one week's time.'

CHAPTER TWO

JOHARA'S MOUTH DROPPED open as Azim's words reverberated through the grand room. *Those* were the first words out of his mouth—not hello, nice to meet you, or any of the other forms of basic introduction acceptable to civilised society? Just this chilling dictate that the clenching of her stomach made her fear she would have no choice but to obey.

'I am glad you are agreeable,' he added shortly, turning away, and Johara realised he'd taken her silence for acquiescence—and was now effectively dismissing her. As far as her future husband was concerned, their conversation was over, and they hadn't even said hello.

'Wait—Your Highness!' Her voice was a hoarse whisper, and Johara cleared her throat, frustrated by her fear. This was too important a moment to act the shocked maiden. Azim turned back to her, his eyes narrowed, his mouth a hard, flat line that looked as if it never saw a smile.

'Yes?'

'It is only...' Johara gulped as she collected her scattered thoughts, the fragments of her dashed hopes. Their conversation—if she could use that word—had been so abrupt she could hardly believe it was over. She hadn't even had a chance to *think*. 'This has all happened so quickly. And we had never met before today—'

'We have met now.'

Johara stared at him, searching for some glimmer of warmth in those starless eyes, a hint of a smile in the uncompromising line of his mouth. She saw neither. 'Yes, but we do not know one another,' she continued, trying to make her tone both light and reasonable. 'And...*marriage*.' She spread her hands, tried for a smile. The pep talk she'd given herself on the plane seemed woefully improbable now, and yet she had no other plans, no other weapon. 'It is a large step to take for two people who have not laid eyes on one another before this moment.'

'Yet one you have, I have been told, been prepared to make for some time. I do not see any reason for your objection now?' The lilt of his voice suggested a question but Johara was wary of answering it. He did not seem as if he was waiting for a response.

When she dared to look into his eyes, she wished she hadn't. They felt like two black holes she could tip right into and fall for ever. 'I only meant...' she tried, 'shouldn't we get to know one another first? In order to—'

Azim's expression did not change a modicum as he answered, cutting her off. 'No.'

Johara took a deep breath, clinging to the remnants of her composure that was now in shreds. Even in her worst imaginings she hadn't expected Azim to be this unrelentingly cold. His expression was pitiless and impatient, his arms folded over his chest, as if she was wasting his time. How could she marry a man such as this? And yet she had to. Her only hope was some kind of negotiation as to the terms.

'Our marriage then will be one of convenience,' she stated.

His mouth twisted, drawing the puckered flesh of the

scar along his cheek tight. 'Surely you had already come to that conclusion.'

'Yes, but I mean...' She faltered, unsure how to present the suggestion that had seemed so logical, so amenable, on the journey here. She had not anticipated Azim al Bahjat's attitude of stony indifference, underlaid by a hostility she didn't understand. Unless she was being paranoid? Perhaps he was like this with everyone. Or perhaps he was simply nervous, as she was.

The prospect was laughable. Azim al Bahjat did not look remotely uncertain or nervous. He was a man utterly in command of the situation—and her. Still Johara persevered. 'Malik and I had discussed—'

'I do not wish to talk about Malik.' Azim's voice was the quiet snick of a drawn blade. 'Do not mention him to me again.'

Johara fell silent, chastened by this dictate. Her father had told her Malik was acting as Azim's advisor, but the lethal warning in his voice made her wonder if their relationship was fraught. Or perhaps it was the relationship with *her* that was fraught. 'I'm sorry. I only meant it would make sense for our marriage to be an arrangement that is convenient to both of us.'

'Make sense?' For a moment Azim looked coldly amused. 'How so?'

Encouraged by the mere fact that he'd asked a question, Johara plunged into her explanation. 'As you might know, I have spent most of my life in France. I am not as familiar with Alazar as you are—'

'You are Alazaran-born, with your bloodline able to be traced back nearly a thousand years.'

Yes, she knew of her precious ancestry, descended hundreds of years ago from the sister of a sultan. 'All I meant is,' she explained, 'France is my home, and has been since

I was a young child. I've only been to Alazar a handful of times in my whole life.'

Azim's mouth twisted in contempt. 'A notable lack in your upbringing. You will have to familiarise yourself with its customs immediately.'

This wasn't going at all the way she'd intended. *Hoped.* 'What I mean to say is,' Johara tried yet again, 'I would like to live in France for as much of the year as possible. Of course, I would come to Alazar when needed, for state functions and the like.' She spoke quickly, tripping over her words, desperate to come to an agreement. 'Whenever I'm needed, of course. It seems a suitable arrangement to us both—'

'Does it?' Azim cocked his head, his narrowed gaze sweeping over her, a dark searchlight. 'It does not seem so to me. Far from it, in fact.'

Frustrations warred with despair and Johara clenched her fists, hiding them in the stiff skirts of her dress. 'May I ask why?'

'My wife belongs with me, not pursuing her own interests in another country,' Azim stated, a hint of a sneer in his voice. 'The Sultana of Alazar must be by the Sultan's side, or in the palace, showing the country what an exemplary, modest and honourable woman she is. That is where you belong, Sadiyyah Behwar,' he finished in a ringing, final tone of a judge delivering his sentence. 'By my side, in the palace harem—or in my bed.'

Azim noted the way Johara's pupils flared even as her face paled. Was she disgusted by the thought of sharing his bed? He'd had his fair share of women over the years, and they had all been more than willing to be there. In any case it didn't matter whether Johara was or not. He was not looking for companionship or even pleasure from this arrangement. After a lifetime of being denied such things, he had schooled himself not to want them.

'You are very blunt,' she managed, two bright spots of colour now visible high on each cheekbone, the delicate skin around her pouty mouth nearly white.

'I am merely stating facts.'

Johara shook her head slowly. 'So you want me with you all the time, and yet you have no interest in getting to know me?'

'What is there to know?' Azim returned. The pain in his temples was becoming too much to indulge her in such a sentimental conversation. He didn't care about her feelings, or even his own. This was a matter of state, nothing more. 'You are young, healthy and eminently suitable,' he clarified. 'You can trace your bloodline back almost as far as I can. That is all I need to know.'

She lifted her chin, her eyes flaring now with anger. Arif had assured him his daughter was extremely biddable, but from this conversation alone Azim knew the man had exaggerated—and her defiance was both an aggravation and an insult he didn't need.

'There must be a dozen women like me,' she said, her chin lifted, 'with suitable breeding and bloodlines. Why are you so determined to marry a stranger you don't even want to get to know?'

Because she'd been intended for Malik. Because choosing anyone else when his entire country had been expecting her as Sultana would be an admission of failure, a sign of defeat, and something he refused to consider. He had suffered too much, sacrificed too much, to fail in this. 'You are my chosen Sultana,' he stated coldly. 'Most women would consider that an honour.'

Her eyes flashed. 'But I am not most women.'

'So I am beginning to realise.'

'I just don't understand—'

'You don't need to understand,' Azim snapped. He took a steadying breath, pain stabbing his temples once more. He could feel a full-fledged migraine coming on, the black spots starting to dance before his eyes, the nausea churning in his stomach. He had five minutes, if that, to get to a dark, quiet room and wait out the agony. 'All you need to do,' he stated in a tone of utter finality, 'is to obey.'

Her mouth dropped open as Azim turned away. He walked blindly from the room, his vision starting to grey at the edges. He could not manage any more. From behind him he heard a ragged gasp.

'Your Highness…' It was a cross between a protest and a plea, a sorrowful sound that grated on his nerves even as it plucked at the broken strings of his compassion. He had been abrupt with his fiancée, he could acknowledge that. If he hadn't been in pain, if he hadn't seen her shudder…perhaps things might have been a little different. But it was too late now to make amends, if he even wanted to, which he didn't think he did. Better for his bride to accept the hard reality, just as he'd had to do time and time again. Life was hard. People turned on you, betrayed you, used you. She could learn the same life lessons he had, albeit in far more comfortable circumstances.

'An attendant will show you to your room,' he stated, forcing the words out past the pain that was building like a towering wall in his head. 'You may spend the next few days preparing for our wedding.' He didn't wait to hear her reply. He knew Arif would force her to comply, and in any case he didn't trust himself to stay standing for much longer. He pushed through the doors, doubling over the moment they'd swung behind him, his hands braced on his knees.

'Your Highness…' An attendant hurried forward, and

with immense effort Azim straightened, throwing off the servant's arm. He couldn't be seen as weak, not even by a servant.

'I'm fine,' he grated. Then he walked on leaden legs to his bedroom, and its welcoming darkness.

Johara stood in the audience chamber for a full five minutes before she felt composed enough to leave its privacy for the prying eyes of the many palace staff. The abruptness of her conversation with Azim had bordered on the surreal, and yet it had possessed the stomach-clenching realisation of hard reality. This man, who had not spared her so much as an introduction, who barked commands, whose smile seemed cruel, was going to be her husband.

She tried to find one redeeming quality in the man she was meant to spend her life with and came up empty. He possessed a strong sense of duty, she supposed, her thoughts laced with desperation and flat-out panic. He wasn't bad-looking; in fact, if his expression hadn't been so severe, his manner so terse, she might have thought him quite handsome. His form was certainly powerful, and even in the shock and tension of their conversation she'd noticed his muscled shoulders, the dark slashes of his eyebrows.

He had a compelling look about him, possessing the kind of bearing that made you want to both stare and look away at the same time. He was too much. Too hard, too cold, too cruel. He hadn't offered her one simple civility in their first meeting. What on earth would their life together look like?

She *couldn't* marry him.

Johara pressed her hands to her cheeks, distantly noting their iciness, as she gazed out of the arched window at the desert vista. A hard blue sky and an unrelenting sun framed the endless, undulating desert. Looking at it hurt Johara's eyes, and made her long for the rolling hills and lavender fields of Provence, the dear familiarity of her book-lined bedroom, her kitchen garden with its pots of herbs, the stillroom where she'd pottered about experimenting with salves and tinctures, pursuing her interest in natural medicine. Made her wish, yet again, that everything about her meeting with Azim had been different. Better. Or preferably, hadn't happened at all.

She dropped her hands and took a deep breath. What recourse did she have now? She was powerless, a woman in a man's world, a sultan's world. Her only option was to run to her father and beg him to release her. Hope flickered faintly as she considered this.

Her father loved her, she knew he did. Yes, he'd been planning for her marriage to the Sultan of Alazar for years, but...he *loved* her. Perhaps her father had not realised what kind of man Azim was. Perhaps when she told him just how cold and hard her husband-to-be seemed, he'd renegotiate yet again. Or at least ask for a delay, months or even years...

Taking a deep breath, Johara turned from the room. A palace attendant was waiting by the door as she came through. 'His Highness wished me to show you your rooms.'

'Thank you, but I'd like to see my father first.'

The attendant's face was blank, his voice polite as he answered, 'Many pardons, but that is not possible.'

The anxiety that had been coiling in her stomach like a serpent about to strike reared up, hissing. 'What do you mean? Why can I not see my own father?'

'He is in a meeting, Sadiyyah Behwar,' the man answered smoothly. 'But I will, of course, let him know you wish to speak with him.'

Johara nodded, the panic receding a little. Perhaps she was overreacting, seeing conspiracy or coercion at every turn. Her father would surely come to her when he was able. He would listen to her. He would understand. He might be ambitious and sometimes a little bit hard, but she had never, not once, doubted his love for her. 'Thank you.'

She followed the man silently down a long marble corridor to a suite of rooms nearly as opulent as the audience chamber where she'd met Azim. She gazed round at all the luxury, the huge bed on its own dais with silk and satin covers, the sunken marble tub in a bathroom that was nearly as large as her bedroom at home, the spacious balcony that overlooked the palace's lush gardens. It was lovely, but all she could see was a gilded prison, invisible bars that would hold her there for the rest of her life.

What would she *do* here, as Azim's wife? Lie on a bed with her face to the wall, as her mother had these many years, trapped by her own endless despair? Johara resisted that with a deep, frightened instinct. She had long ago vowed never to be like her mother, had chosen a cheerful, optimistic approach to life as a matter of principle, because to give in to doubt or despair was no life at all. Yet optimism was hard to find now.

So then would she devote herself to her children, if they came, and try to forget the unending loneliness of being yoked to a man who had no interest in her beyond her bloodline? Would she be able to make friends, make a *life*? There was so much she didn't know, so much she couldn't imagine and didn't even want to imagine. She wanted more for her life than what Azim was offering. She wanted more for her life than any arranged marriage could provide. It had taken a fleeting week of precious freedom to make her realise that.

She sank onto a divan by the window, her body aching with both emotional and physical fatigue. It had been a little more than twelve hours since her father had told her she was marrying Azim. And only a week until she would be forced to say her vows...unless she could find some way out of this disaster—seek her father and try to persuade him to end the engagement. He had to listen to her. He loved her, she reminded herself. She was his *habibti*, his treasure, his little pearl. He wouldn't let her suffer a fate such as this.

Azim blinked in the gloom of his bedchamber, the migraine having finally lessened to a dull, endurable throb, the fragments of a dream still piercing his brain in poignant shards. He'd been back in Naples, hiding from Paolo, cowering and afraid. He hated that dream. He hated how it made him feel.

With determined effort Azim shook it off, banishing the memories of his confusion and fear. He was a sultan-in-waiting now, restored to his rightful place, a man of power and authority. He would not allow himself to be bested by his old nightmares, even if he'd had more and more of them since returning to Alazar.

He had no idea what time it was, but he noted the moonlight sliding between the shutters and knew it had been many hours. He closed his eyes, his whole body aching with the effort of having battled the pain—and won.

The headaches that had plagued him since he was fourteen years old had been getting worse since he'd returned to Alazar, no doubt from the unrelieved tension of being back in a place with so many bitter memories, as well as his legacy hanging by no more than a slender thread. He hated the fragility of his position, the powerlessness it made him feel. No wonder he'd had that old dream. He had no idea if the old tribes of the desert would accept him as a leader when he had been gone from his country, from his people's memory, for so long. He had only been a boy when he'd been taken, an event he couldn't actually remember. He had not yet had a chance to prove himself capable and worthy of command, no matter that his grandfather had been preparing him for it for years. Marrying Johara, as unwilling as she was, would help to cement his position as the next Sultan. He needed her compliance...or at least her perceived compliance. How she felt didn't matter at all as long as she obeyed.

Sighing heavily, he rose from his bed, the room seesawing around him until he was able to blink it back into balanced focus. It wasn't only the pressures and tenuousness of his role that weighed on him now. It was the look of shocked hurt in Johara's clear grey eyes when he'd issued his flat commands earlier that day. He had not attempted to soften them with the merest modicum of kindness or compassion; he'd been in too much pain as well as too angry at her own unguarded reaction, when she'd looked up at the palace and he alone had seen the truth in her face.

He supposed he would need to remedy the situation somehow, but he was not a man prone to apologies. In the world he inhabited an apology was weakness, the admission of any guilt a mistake. He could not afford to do that now, even if he wanted to, which he did not. It was better for his new bride not to have any expectations except obedience.

'Azim?' Malik spoke softly from behind the bedroom door. Quickly Azim grabbed his shirt and pulled it on. He'd shucked it off in the worst throes of the migraine, when he'd been covered in icy sweat, but he was always careful to keep his back covered. No one, not even his infrequent lovers, had seen his scars. No one would know of his shame.

He flicked on the lights even though the flash of brightness sliced through his head like a laser. He straightened his clothes and ran a hand over his closely cropped hair, determined that Malik not see any sign of his weakness.

'Enter.'

Malik came in, closing the door quietly behind him. 'You are well?'

'Yes, of course. What is it?' He spoke more tersely than he'd intended, and saw the flash of bruised recognition in his brother's eyes. Once, a lifetime ago, they'd been close, leaning on each other when the adults in their lives had failed them, but now Azim had no idea how to navigate that old, once-precious relationship. For too long everyone had felt like an enemy, someone who would break the trust he now refused to give.

'You spoke to Johara?'

'Yes. She is not as compliant as her father indicated.'

Malik leaned one powerful shoulder against the doorframe, his arms folded. 'She knows her duty.'

'I would hope so.' Azim reached for his trousers, preferring the Western dress he was far more comfortable in after twenty years in Italy, at least in private. 'I told her we would marry in a week's time.'

Malik's eyebrows rose. 'So soon?'

'I do not have time to waste.'

'Still, that is rather quick,' Malik said mildly. 'Considering only a week ago she was meant to marry me.'

'She was meant,' Azim clarified with clipped precision, 'to marry the heir to the Sultanate, whoever that was.'

Malik inclined his head. 'You are right, of course. But she is very young, and she is not as used to our ways as you might—'

'I thought you did not know her.' Azim heard the edge to his voice and turned away from his brother. The knowledge that Johara had been meant for Malik gave him a deep-seated sense of resentment that he did not fully understand. He knew Malik and Johara had never so much as kissed, and yet still he resisted the notion of them together. So much had been taken from him, including his bride. He was more determined than ever to gain it all back, no matter what the cost—or who paid the price.

'She said she has spent most of her time in France,' he remarked to Malik. 'Why is that?'

Malik shrugged. 'Her mother has been ill for a long time. Arif has kept her away from Alazar.'

'Simply because she is ill? That does not seem sensible.'

'I am not quite sure of the details,' Malik answered. 'Arif never speaks of her.' He paused. 'That seems intentional.'

Azim frowned. 'I was assured Johara's bloodline was impeccable—'

'It is. But even impeccable bloodlines contain people with problems, with illness or suffering.'

Azim did not answer. God knew he had his own share of suffering, and he was descended from kings. 'Well,' he said after a moment. 'She will comply. She has no choice.'

'A little kindness might go a long way,' Malik suggested mildly. 'Considering her youth and inexperience.'

Azim had come to that conclusion himself, but he didn't particularly like hearing it from Malik. And what kindness could he offer her? He had no time or interest, not to mention ability, in wooing, paying court or offering flattery. He was a man of action, not words. He always had been. And in the world he'd lived in these last twenty years, flattery got you nowhere.

'I can manage my own bride,' he told Malik, his tone curt. Malik nodded, his mouth a pressed line. Tension simmered between them. Once they'd been as close as brothers could be, sharing everything, including sorrow, and now—what? Reluctant allies, perhaps, but even that was a step of faith for him, a level of trust he wasn't comfortable with, not even with Malik.

After Malik had left Azim summoned an attendant to his room. 'Send some fabric to Sadiyyah Behwar,' he instructed. 'Brocade and satin, spare no expense. As a gift from me, for her wedding dress. And ensure there are seamstresses on hand to do her bidding.' He knew she already possessed a gown from her intended wedding to Malik, but he wanted her to have a new one, one that was just for him. A new start for a new marriage. He hoped Johara appreciated his gesture.

CHAPTER THREE

JOHARA WRAPPED HER arms around herself, suppressing a shiver despite the sultry summer air, as she looked out on the steep roofs and steeples of Paris's Latin Quarter. She'd arrived back in Nice that morning and she was still trying to ignore the icy panic creeping coldly over her—and to convince herself that she'd made the right decision.

In the end it had been both easy and heartbreaking. She closed her eyes against the look of icy disbelief in her father's eyes when she'd asked him to delay the wedding. The memory of the conversation caused pain to lance through her again.

'F-F-F… Father,' she'd stammered, inwardly cringing at the look of barely concealed impatience in her father's face. She'd caught him leaving a meeting, and the other diplomats and dignitaries had eyed her with cold disapproval, a woman trying to break into a man's world.

'What are you doing here, Johara?' Arif asked. He glanced back at his colleagues. 'She is to marry His Highness Azim next week.'

'That's what I wanted to talk about,' Johara said, trying to gather the tattered remnants of her courage. 'About the marriage…'

'What is it?' Arif grabbed her elbow and steered her to a private alcove. 'You are humiliating me in public,' he snapped, his eyes narrowed to dark slits, everything in him radiating icy disapproval. Johara shrank back, shocked. He'd never looked at her like this back in France, even when she'd dared to risk his displeasure.

'Azim is…very cold.'

'Cold?' Arif looked nonplussed.

'He seems almost cruel,' Johara whispered, losing courage by the second. 'I…I don't want to marry him. I can't!'

Arif stared at her, his lips thinned, the skin around them white. 'Clearly I have spoiled you,' he stated in a hard voice. 'For you to be speaking this way to me now.'

'Father, please—'

'You have been petted and indulged your whole life,' Arif cut her off. 'And I have asked only one thing of you, something that is a great honour and privilege. And now you tell me to humiliate myself and my family, risk my career and livelihood, because you find him a little cold?' He shook his head slowly. 'I will do my best to pretend this conversation has not happened.'

'But, Father, if you love me…' Johara began, her voice shaking. 'Then surely you wouldn't…'

'Nothing about this has to do with love,' Arif stated. 'It has to do with duty and honour. Never forget that, Johara. Love is a facile emotion for fools and weaklings. Your mother is a testament to that.' Without waiting for her reply he stalked off, leaving her reeling.

Love is a facile emotion. She could hardly believe he'd dismissed her concerns, her feelings so easily. And worse, seemed to have none of his own. Like a naïve child she'd believed her father loved her. Now she knew the terrible truth that he didn't, and never had.

Baubles, presents, a careless pat or smile—these things cost her father nothing. They'd been sops to appease her, not expressions of his love. It was so obvious now, so awful.

For when his ambition was at stake, Johara's happiness was a sacrifice he didn't even have to think about making.

Her father had arranged her flight back to Provence that afternoon, so she could pack her things and collect her mother before returning for the wedding. Naima Behwar rarely left her bed, much less the villa in Provence, and Arif didn't want the trouble of having to coax her out of either. Amazing, really, how Johara could now see how self-serving he was. Kindness only came when it was free. Why hadn't she considered his father's treatment of her mother—his indifference and impatience—as a true reflection of his character, rather than the presents and smiles he carelessly tossed her way? Why had she been so stupid and shallow?

All during the flight to Nice her mind had raced in hopeless circles, trying to find a way out. A way forward. She was by nature an optimist, but her innate cheerfulness had taken a critical hit. She'd barely been able to summon a smile for the chauffeur, Thomas, who'd met her at the airport; he had been in the family's employ for two decades, and had once taught her to ride a bicycle. His wife Lucille had worked as their cook and first showed Johara how to distil oil from plants, the beginning of her interest in natural medicine. She'd miss them both, and the quiet, simple contentment of the life she'd had, the life she realised now she'd taken for granted.

Then, while Thomas had been getting the car, Johara had made a split-second decision, acting on desperate impulse, something she never did. She'd run.

Her mind had been a blur of panic as she'd walked away from where Thomas had told her to wait, towards the shuttle bus that went to the train station in Nice Ville. Within an hour she'd been on a train to Paris, amazed that she'd actually done it. She'd run away. She'd freed herself.

And now that she'd booked into a shabby, anonymous-looking hotel on a side alley in the Latin Quarter, she wondered what on earth she was going to do next. She had her freedom, but she knew she was ill-equipped to deal with it. Taking the train and navigating the crowded streets of Paris by herself had already felt overwhelming, more than she'd ever dealt with before. How was she going to survive, get a job, make a life for herself?

And, she wondered with a shiver that this time she couldn't suppress, how was she going to keep from being found? She shuddered to think of both her father and her husband-to-be's reactions when they learned she'd run. Perhaps they already knew. Thomas, their driver, had probably already sounded the alarm.

Outside a church bell began to toll and a flock of sparrows rose in a dark flurry. Laughter from the streets below floated up, and all the sounds and sights, the sheer normalcy of them, lightened Johara's spirits a little.

She could do this. She *would* do this. How hard could it be, to find some menial job that would keep a roof over her head and food on the table? Her needs were small and although she didn't have much life experience she knew she was smart as well as a quick learner. Surely any life, no matter how small, was better than being forced into a marriage she didn't want. Taking a deep breath, she turned from the window and went to get ready to look for a job.

Fifteen minutes later she was easing her way along the crowded streets of the Latin Quarter, clutching her bag to her chest as people moved past her in an indifferent stream. She hadn't realised how noisy and crowded the city was. Her few experiences of Paris had been from behind the tinted windows of a limousine, and then she'd been ushered into one boutique or another with her mother, everything exclusive and private. And even those trips had been a long time ago—her mother had not roused herself to go to Paris, or anywhere, in years.

Spotting a sign for a small café, Johara decided to take the necessary plunge. She ducked into the tiny restaurant and stammered a question to the hassled-looking manager by the kitchen door, asking if he was hiring.

'Do you have any waitressing experience?' he asked, his voice full of scepticism as he eyed her up and down.

'No, but—'

'Sorry, no.'

Dejectedly she turned away. She repeated the same cringing experience in the next four cafés. All of the managers had looked at her with either doubt or disbelief when she'd asked for work, and Johara wondered how they could tell she was inexperienced. Was it the way she dressed? Spoke? Or was her naiveté that obvious, like a beacon above her head?

Her feet ached and her stomach rumbled—she hadn't eaten since she'd been on the plane hours ago. Worse than either of those afflictions was the plunging sense of despair that she wasn't going to be able to make it in the real world. And what would she do then? Slink back to Azim with her tail tucked firmly between her legs, her head lowered in guilty remorse, and accept a cold, loveless marriage with a man she didn't like or even know?

No. She would rather pound every street in Paris looking for work than submit to a man as cold and cruel as Azim al Bahjat.

'*Salut, chérie,*' a man's low, purring voice carried over the sounds of the crowd, and Johara turned, startled to realise he was talking to her.

'*Salut,*' she said cautiously. The man's smile was wide as he lounged in the doorway of the shabbiest café Johara had ever seen, just a few tiny, dirty tables on a floor of cracked tiles.

'Are you looking for work?' He made a moue of sympathy. 'Finding it difficult?'

'A bit,' Johara admitted. 'Why?' She nodded to the café. 'Are you hiring?'

The man's smile widened. 'As it happens, yes. Do you know how to be nice to customers?'

It seemed a strange question, and Johara shrugged. 'I think so.'

The man eyed her up and down in a way that made her blush and shift uncomfortably, her bag clutched to her chest. 'Then you can start tonight. Can you be back here at nine?'

Johara swallowed, hardly daring to believe that she'd actually found a job. She didn't particularly like the look of the greasy man or the shabby café, but she was hardly in a position to choose. 'Yes, of course.'

Back at the hotel she ate, showered and changed, trying to ignore the sense of unease she felt about the man and his offer of work. As she headed out into the sultry summer evening butterflies flitted in her stomach and she tried to walk as she saw other women walking, with their heads tilted at a proud angle, their hips swaying, as if they knew who they were and where they were going. Johara felt as if she knew neither and had no idea how to find out.

The café was full of noisy customers when she approached, relieved that she'd managed to get herself to the right place. So many of the narrow, cobbled streets of the Latin Quarter looked the same. The same beady-eyed man who had hired her met her at the doorway.

'Ah, *chérie*. I'm so glad you came.' He drew her by the hand into the hot press of people, one arm snaking around her waist. Alarm bells started clanging in Johara's head as she tensed, her body arching instinctively away from him. No man had ever touched her so intimately, their hips bumping, her breasts brushing his shoulder.

'Don't be shy,' he said with a laugh, pulling her closer, one hand brushing her breast. 'Remember I said you had to be nice.'

Johara glanced around at the crowded café, and all the faces looked sweaty and leering. The man's hand was still on her waist, the side of her body pressed tightly to his. The acrid smell of alcohol and sweat stung her nostrils and made her head swim.

She opened her mouth to say something, to explain this wasn't quite what she'd thought it would be, but no words came out. And then someone else was speaking.

'Get your hands off her right now.' The words were clipped, the tone utterly lethal. The sneering smile on the man's face slid right off when he caught sight of whoever was standing behind Johara. He held up his hands as he backed away.

'*Pardon, monsieur*, I didn't know she was taken.'

'Now you know.'

Slowly Johara turned, her heart beating so hard she could feel the blood roaring in her ears. It couldn't be... but of course it was. Azim stood in the doorway of the café, his eyes blazing black fire, his hands clenched into fists at his sides. With his powerful frame, the scar snaking down his cheek and his air of barely leashed fury, he was utterly terrifying. No wonder the man backed away. She wanted to run.

'Don't think of trying it,' Azim said in a low, dangerous voice, and Johara knew he'd read her thoughts.

'How did you find me?' she asked in a shaky whisper.

'Easily. Come with me. Now.' As his strong, lean fingers circled her wrist and pulled her towards him Johara had no choice but to comply. She stumbled as he drew her from the café, throwing one hand out to the doorframe to keep from falling.

'Stop, you're hurting me.'

Azim slowed, his fingers loosening around her wrist, even as his expression remained icily furious.

'My car is waiting.'

'I'm not going with you.' Johara wished she'd sounded more firm.

'Don't be ridiculous,' Azim snapped. 'You can't stay here.'

'Why not?'

'Because,' he gritted between clenched teeth, stepping closer to her, 'I just took you out of a whorehouse.'

'A…' Her jaw dropped.

'You do know what that is?' Azim inquired. 'I presume you're not that innocent?'

A fiery blush rose from her throat to the crown of her head. 'Yes, I know what that is,' Johara muttered. 'I've read books.'

'Oh, well, then. You're the voice of experience, I suppose.' He shook his head, clearly disgusted, and pulled her, gently at least, towards the waiting limousine. This time Johara went without a murmur.

She clambered into the luxurious interior, the leather sumptuous and soft against her bare legs. Azim climbed in next to her and barked out an address to the driver before slamming the door and leaning back against the seat.

Realisations were firing through Johara, short-circuiting her synapses. 'Was it really…?' she began through trembling lips.

'Yes,' Azim stated flatly. 'It was.'

Her teeth started to chatter as she realised how close she'd come to utter disaster. She could have been raped.

She could have been sold into sexual slavery. She could
have been... She closed her eyes as a wave of nausea hit
her. She could hardly bear to think of it.

'Are you cold?' Azim demanded, and Johara shook her
head. She wasn't cold, but she couldn't seem to stop shaking.

He eyed her for a moment, his expression utterly fierce,
before he reached forward to the limo's minibar and poured
a generous shot of whisky into a glass. 'Here. Drink this.
It will help.'

Her numb fingers curled around the glass. 'Help...?'

'You're in shock.'

She glanced down at the amber liquid, its pungent smell
making her grimace. 'I've never drunk hard alcohol before.'

'Now is as good a time as any.' Azim watched her, his
very gaze commanding her to drink, and Johara raised
the glass to her lips.

The whisky burned down her throat and lit a fire in
her belly. Somehow she managed not to sputter, but she
wiped her mouth with the back of her hand, thrusting the
glass back at Azim.

'No more.'

A tiny smile curved his mouth, making his scar pucker.
'Not bad for the first time. You didn't cough.'

'I wanted to.'

'You have strength of spirit.' From his tone she couldn't
tell if that was a good or bad thing.

She turned to look out of the window, unsettled by the
sudden and overwhelming turn of events. Outside the limo
the streets of Paris streamed by in an electric blur.

'Where are we going?' she asked after a few tense, silent minutes had ticked by.

'To my flat.'

'How did you find me? Easily, I know, but…'

'Your driver alerted your father, who told me.'

So her father had betrayed her yet again. She wasn't surprised, but it still hurt. 'Was he angry?'

'Furious,' Azim answered shortly. 'What did you expect?'

For someone who loved her to think about her happiness. But of course her father had never really loved her. How long, she wondered, was that going to hurt? 'I don't know,' she mumbled. She felt tired and near tears, trapped and humiliated, as if she were a naughty child being marched to the corner.

'Even I did not think you would be so stupid and selfish as to run away,' Azim said. Anger thrummed through his voice. 'Even though you had made it clear what you thought of our forthcoming marriage.'

'As did you,' Johara returned, half amazed by her own audacity. She never spoke to her father, or anyone, like this. It felt good to speak her mind to someone, even if she'd regret it later.

'So I did.' Azim was silent for a moment and Johara found herself suddenly conscious of his nearness, the powerful length of his thigh brushing hers on the seat. She could smell his aftershave, the mingled aromas of sandalwood and cedar. Her senses stirred in a way that felt unfamiliar and intriguing. She had a bizarre desire to shift closer, to feel the length of his leg against her own, a prospect that horrified her. This man was her enemy. He was also, unless she managed a miracle, going to be her husband.

Azim turned to look out of the window, his gaze hooded as he looked out at the blur of traffic. 'Our first meeting,' he said finally, 'did not go as I had intended.'

'Oh? What had you intended?' She was curious but she

couldn't keep a sarcastic edge from her voice. Disconcerted now by his nearness, she found the memory of their first conversation—such as it had been—still stung. How had he thought any sane woman would respond to his unemotional, autocratic dictates?

'That you would be the compliant woman your father indicated that you were,' he replied as he turned back to her. 'But so far you have disappointed me at every turn.'

'And you have disappointed me,' Johara snapped, and then drew a ragged breath, pressing herself against the seat, as she realised from the look of cold fury on Azim's face that she'd gone too far.

'Then we shall both have to learn to live with disappointment,' he answered after a moment, his voice dangerously even. 'Hardly a tragedy.' He turned his head away once more and they did not talk again until the limo had stopped in front of an elegant building off the Champs-élysées.

'Is there where you live?'

'It is one of my homes.' The driver opened the door and Azim slid out, extending a hand back towards Johara. With the awkward angle of the seat, as well as Azim's body barring the door, she had no choice but to take it.

The slide of his strong hand against hers was an unexpected jolt, as if she'd touched a live wire. Shocked by the sensation, she let out a gasp, and then registered Azim's cool smile of satisfaction with wary confusion.

The smile disappeared as soon as she'd noted it, their gazes locking in a taut battle of wills before Azim dropped her hand and turned towards the building. On legs as shaky as the rest of her, Johara followed.

CHAPTER FOUR

A THOUSAND THOUGHTS and feelings whirled through Azim as he stalked through the foyer of the apartment building, ignoring the concierge's murmured pleasantries. Foremost was fury, that Johara had shamed him in such a way by publicly absconding days before their marriage. After that came disgust, that he'd led her to do such a thing. As angry as he was about her runaway attempt, he knew he'd handled their first meeting badly. He just didn't know if he had it in him to make amends.

Beyond those two negative emotions was a deep-seated relief that he'd saved Johara from, at best, a very unpleasant evening, and at worst, a lifetime of enforced prostitution—and then finally primal, masculine satisfaction, for in the moment when their hands had touched he'd felt her reaction, like a spark travelling up his arm, igniting in his belly. She desired him.

Perhaps she didn't want to, perhaps she didn't even realise it, but he knew. He'd seen it in the flare of her pupils, heard it in her surprised gasp and felt it in the shudder that had gone through her, just as he'd felt his own body's response. Their marriage, then, would at least have sexual chemistry—and that was no small thing.

They didn't speak in the tiny, enclosed space of the antique lift that juddered up towards the penthouse. Johara pressed herself against the grate, her grey eyes startlingly wide and looking almost silver in the dim light. He'd seen her only in the shapeless robes, and now he noted the slender and enticing curves highlighted by the sundress she wore. The thin, gauzy material clung to her small, pert breasts and tiny waist, flaring out about her long, slender legs. No wonder that disgusting pimp had wanted her for his whorehouse. She was gorgeous, innocence and sensuality in one jaw-dropping package, and she didn't even realise how alluring she was.

'Does your father know you wear clothes like these?' he demanded and Johara pressed back even farther away from him.

'My father lets me wear what I like.'

Wasn't around to notice or care, Azim filled in silently. He'd taken Arif's measure at their first meeting; the older man had been more than eager to have his daughter exchange grooms weeks before the wedding. While it suited Azim's purposes admirably, it did not endear him to the man. He was the worst combination of weakness and lust for power, just as Caivano had been. It had led to his tormentor's downfall, and it would eventually lead to Arif's. He would not have such a man in his cabinet.

The lift jolted to a stop and the doors opened. Azim ushered Johara out to his flat, a soaring, open space that took up the entire top floor of the building.

Johara stepped out, craning her neck to take in the vaulted ceiling and huge windows. The doors of the lift closed behind Azim and he stood watching her, noticing the way her dress clung to her hips, the fabric whispering about her shapely legs as she moved. A dark, curling tendril of hair lay against the nape of her neck and he had the absurd urge to lift it and see the delicate skin beneath.

She turned to face him, her trembling lips pressed together, her chin raised in challenge. Even though her rebellion tried him sorely, he could not help but admire her courage. He hadn't thought she'd possessed the audacity to make a run for it. He was, perversely and annoyingly, pleased that she'd been that daring, even if he was still furious that she'd tried.

'So?' Johara asked, her voice managing to be both strident and shaky at the same time. 'What now?'

Azim folded his arms. 'You will marry me.'

'Of course.' She let out a high, trembling laugh. 'Of course, I have no say in the matter.'

Irritation, and something deeper and rawer, rippled through him. 'If I am not mistaken, you have known about your arranged marriage for nearly your whole life. Why are you resisting now?'

'Because.' Johara looked away and said nothing more.

Azim regarded her coolly. 'Because of me, you mean.'

She shot him one wild glance before turning away again, giving him a view of her profile, the high forehead, the smooth curve of her cheek, the heavy mass of hair pulled back in an elegant chignon. 'You have made your intentions clear,' she said. 'You have no interest in getting to know me.'

'Did Malik?' He hadn't wanted to mention his brother, hated even thinking about Johara married to him, sharing his bed. Quickly Azim banished the image. 'Well?' he demanded when Johara did not answer. 'Did he?'

Johara glared at him, the lift of her chin now seeming stubborn rather than courageous, and entirely aggravating. 'Not particularly,' she said after a moment, the words drawn from her reluctantly and yet ringing with stark honesty.

'Well, then.' Azim didn't know what point he'd been trying to prove. That his bride-to-be objected to wedding him more than his brother? That she was repelled by him, by the scar on his face? What would she think if she saw the scars on the rest of his body? Not, of course, that she ever would.

'If I'm honest,' Johara said after a moment, her voice quiet, 'I wasn't looking forward to marrying Malik, either. What woman wants to marry a stranger for the sake of a crown?'

'I imagine there are many.'

'I am not one of them.'

'But you agreed.' He cocked his head. 'Your father insisted on that.'

'He would.' A new bitterness spiked her words and she looked away again. 'I agreed because I've known nothing else. Because...' She shook her head, clearly not wanting to say more.

'If you were so reluctant, why did you not say something to my brother?'

'I just didn't want to think of it. I... I pretended it wasn't going to happen and I told myself I could carry on with my life as normal afterwards. It was easier to do that, since I hardly ever saw him. We only met a couple of times, for no more than a few minutes. And I had my life in France.'

A life she seemed desperate to get back to. Was someone waiting for her there? Perhaps his bride was not as innocent as her father claimed, although considering her obvious naiveté he found that a difficult notion to entertain. 'It seems remarkably shortsighted,' he remarked. 'Your marriage was in a matter of months.'

'I know.' She hunched her shoulders. 'The closer it got, the less I tried to think of it. A child's response, but perhaps I was a child.' Her lips trembled again and to Azim's horror he saw a single, silvery tear slip down her cheek. She dashed it away with a grimace. 'Perhaps I still am.'

'You are not a child.' The response he'd felt in her earlier, the woman's body he saw now, told him as much. 'But you are innocent and have lived a sheltered life. That is not a bad thing.'

'Except that it caused me to walk into a whorehouse tonight, thinking I was going to be a waitress.' Azim saw the glimmer of a smile through her sadness, and felt a flicker of admiration for her bravery, facing a future she didn't want, even as he rebelled against the knowledge that *he* was that future. 'What must you think of me?'

'I think,' he said, his voice low and gravelly, 'that I am very thankful I found you in time.'

Johara closed her eyes, shaking her head. Another tear slipped down her cheek and Azim had an urge to comfort her, an instinct that seemed absurd. He was her captor, the person she was fighting against. Her enemy, or so she seemed to think. How could he comfort her? He'd never comforted anyone.

And yet as he watched her turn to the window, looking out at the wash of lights that was Paris at night, he could not keep from feeling a sharp pang of sympathy for her. He knew what it was like to feel trapped. He'd felt the invisible walls of a prison surrounding him, suffocating him for too many years, just as he suspected she was feeling now.

Johara let out a soft, sorrowful sigh, a sound of resignation and even despair, and the wave of sympathy he'd felt receded. His bride-to-be's prison was luxurious, with every comfort to hand. She was poised to become a woman of respect and power, not some lackey or near-slave. She had nothing to complain about.

'You should rest,' he said, his tone abrupt. She turned back to him, startled and wary. 'Tomorrow is going to be a big day.'

'Why…?'

He shook his head, not willing to say more then. It was time that his future wife started to obey him, no questions asked. 'Go to bed,' he commanded. 'You may have any one of the guest rooms down the hall.' He nodded towards a dark corridor leading away from the open-plan living area. 'And don't even think of trying to escape. The apartment is locked and alarmed, and the doorman has orders not to assist you in any way.'

Johara blinked, clearly shocked by both the information and his tone, and Azim hardened his resolve. Johara had shown him just how loyal she could be. He would not trust her an inch. Considering he'd never trusted anyone, it was hardly a loss. Turning on his heel, he left her alone in the room without waiting to see whether she would obey. He knew she would.

Johara woke to bright sunlight spilling through the tall, sashed windows and for an instant she felt cheerful, her old, optimistic self, intent on a new, sunny day. Then the memories of the last forty-eight hours played on a loop through her brain and she sagged against her pillows, exhausted before the day had begun. She was Azim's prisoner, and soon she would be his wife. Her one desperate bid for freedom had utterly failed. She saw no way to mount another, and Azim seemed utterly determined to marry her.

Did she have any options at all? With a heavy heart Johara ran through the possibilities. She had a feeling it would be near-impossible to run away again, and once she was back in Alazar it would be even harder. And even if she did manage to get away, what would she do? Where would she go? Her one foray into independence had shown her how ill-equipped she was for it.

Her heart heavier than ever, she rose from the bed,

knowing she needed to face the day—and Azim—at some point. Would they fly back to Alazar today? Would she see her father? The thought brought a lightning strike of pain. Her father had shown his true colours. The relationship she'd thought she'd had, that she'd counted on, had never really existed. Her father didn't love her. No one did. The best and only thing she could do was face her future, her chin lifted high.

Last night she'd stumbled into the first bedroom she'd found, smarting from Azim's set-down and aching from the trials of the day. Now she looked around the room properly, admiring its clean lines, the cool colours. A huge window overlooked the city, the Seine winding its green-blue way through the narrow streets and wide boulevards. And her suitcase was by the door.

Johara registered it with a mixture of bemusement and apprehension. Azim had moved quickly in this, as he had with everything else, finding out where she was staying and getting her things. What would he do next? What demand would he make of her?

She showered and dressed slowly, taking her time, wanting to postpone the moment when she opened her bedroom door and faced Azim. Eventually she decided it would be better simply to get it over with, and in any case she was hungry. She came into the living area to find him dressed in a sharply tailored Italian suit, sitting at the dining table with a computer tablet and a cup of coffee. He looked up as she entered the room, and in that second Johara's whole body blazed with an awareness that shocked her, his dark gaze seeming to see right inside her, peel away all her protective layers.

She stopped where she stood, everything tingling from Azim's single, blazing look. Had his cheekbones always been so blade-sharp? Had his lips really been that full? And why on earth was she thinking this way now?

'Are you going to work?' she asked uncertainly, for he looked brisk and businesslike, poised for action. But perhaps he always looked like that. She really didn't know this man at all.

'No.' He nodded towards the silver coffee pot on the table, along with a tray of croissants and pastries. 'You should eat.'

'Are you always going to tell me what to do?' Johara returned, more out of curiosity than pique, and Azim arched an eyebrow.

'Are you not hungry?'

'Yes, but...' She shrugged, not wanting to pick a fight over pastries. She didn't like the way Azim barked out commands, but she supposed she'd have to get used to it. Their impending wedding loomed, a dark cloud on the horizon coming ever closer, impossible to ignore and too big to flee, even if her mind still raced to find possibilities.

Azim sat back in his chair, watching her as she came to the table and poured herself a cup of coffee. She sat down, conscious of his brooding look, the long brown fingers wrapped around his coffee cup. For some reason seeing him this morning, freshly showered and wearing a suit, felt different than before, when she'd been greeting a stranger dressed in ceremonial robes in an opulent room in the palace. As for last night...she'd been so shocked by the turn in events that she'd barely registered what he looked like.

Now she couldn't seem to keep her gaze from darting to him, noting the play of muscles under the crisp white shirt, the steely glint in his fathomless eyes, the barest hint of stubble on his freshly shaven jaw. Each detail imprinted itself on her senses and made it hard to focus. She'd never noticed such things about Malik. Why was she reacting this way to Azim now? Was it simply because her wedding was closer than ever and impossible to ignore—or because Azim seemed more dangerous, more primal than Malik ever had? She could hardly believe they were brothers.

'Is it strange?' she asked abruptly, following the train of her thought without considering the consequences. 'To be back?'

Azim lowered his coffee cup, his eyes narrowing to dark slits. 'Strange? What do you mean?'

Johara shrugged, realising again how little she knew this man. And yet, in that moment, she wanted to know a little more. 'You have been gone from Alazar for a long time.'

'And I'm not in Alazar now.'

'But…you know what I mean.'

Azim rose from the table, taking his computer tablet and slipping it into an expensive-looking leather attaché. 'Yes, it is strange, but only in that it is not strange. If that makes sense to you.'

'I suppose it does.' She paused, toying with her pastry with the tines of her fork. 'My father said you had lost your memory.'

Azim stilled, his hands resting on the attaché. 'Yes.'

She glanced up, saw the wary, almost hunted look on his face and wondered at it. 'Have you gained all your memory back? Of everything?'

'No. Of most things. Most of my childhood, at any rate.' He zipped up the case and straightened, his expression closed now, as if it had been wiped clean.

Johara nodded slowly. She could tell the conversation was over, and yet she was still curious. 'If we are to be married, we should know things about one another,' she blurted.

'If?' Azim repeated with a sardonic lift of one eyebrow. 'There is no if.'

She looked away, hopelessness warring with something else, something indefinable that she didn't recognise, an emotion that stirred inside her like something long dormant coming to life.

'I don't understand why you must marry me and not someone more suitable.'

'There is no one more suitable.'

Johara let out a hollow laugh. 'I am not the only young woman with impressive Alazaran lineage.'

Azim was silent for a moment, his arms folded across his chest, biceps bulging. 'No, but you are the only one who was engaged to my brother,' he said at last.

'Why does that matter?'

'You have been known as the next Sultana for fifteen years. To choose someone else would be to disappoint expectations and sow doubt among my people. I do not wish to do either.'

'Why would they doubt?'

Azim's mouth tightened, his eyes flashing darkly. 'I have been gone a long time.'

So marrying her would help to stabilise the country, or at least his rule. Johara sighed and shook her head. 'It is hard to believe I am that important.'

'Be flattered,' Azim returned dryly.

'I would rather be free.'

Something flashed across his face, so quickly that Johara almost missed it. She thought it might be pity, or perhaps compassion. As if he understood what she meant, how she felt. But she could tell by the iron set of his jaw and the steel in his eyes that any momentary flicker of compassion would not change his decision or set her free.

'You have had plenty of time to get used to the idea of

an arranged marriage,' Azim said with a dismissive flick of his fingers. 'And in any case, if you did not marry me, what would you do? Where would you go?' She stared at him mutely, not wanting to admit how few options she had, but Azim didn't need her to answer anyway. 'You almost stumbled into a life of prostitution when you'd only been on your own for a few hours,' he continued, his tone reminding her of the relentless growl of a steamroller, flattening every argument, every opposition. 'You are not suited for work, and you have very little experience of the world. You have no choice.'

'How can you say I am not suited for work?' Johara protested. 'You don't know me.'

Azim shrugged. 'I admit I assume, but have you ever done a day's work?'

She spent hours in her garden and stillroom in France, or in her bedroom studying books on herbal and natural medicine. Maybe that wasn't the same as an eight-hour shift working as a waitress, but she resented the implication that she was lazy or spoiled. Still she said nothing, because to trot out her list of meagre accomplishments now felt both pathetic and pointless. Azim had already told her he wasn't interested in getting to know her beyond her bloodline and breeding.

'I have very little experience of this world,' she said, addressing his second point, 'and I am unlikely to get more stuck in a palace, hardly ever able to go out.'

'Now you are the one making assumptions.'

'Am I? You told me yourself that my only place was by your side, in the harem, or...' She trailed off, her cheeks going pink as she realised the trap she'd stupidly set for herself, and then walked right into.

'Or in my bed,' Azim filled in, his voice a soft, beguiling purr. 'There are worse places to be than those.'

'I wouldn't know,' Johara muttered, looking away. She was utterly out of her depth.

'No, you wouldn't,' Azim agreed in that same quiet voice. He had prowled as stealthily as a panther up to her chair, close enough so she could breathe in the sandalwood-and-cedar scent of his aftershave. 'But that is at least one area of marriage that could prove interesting to us both.'

Her breath came out in a shaky rush. 'Interesting…?'

'Pleasurable.' One hand reached down to her own nerve-less fingers and drew her up so she was facing him, their bodies only inches apart. Unable to bear the look of sensual intensity on his face, Johara looked down, conscious of his fingers twined with hers, his body so close she could feel the heat rolling off him. She'd never been so close to a man before. If she moved so much as an inch, she'd be touching him. Her head swam.

'Perhaps we should see how pleasurable,' he suggested softly. 'So we are not taken by surprise on our wedding night.'

'I don't…' Johara found she couldn't say anything else. Her head felt as if it were full of cotton wool, and yet every sense was achingly, exquisitely alive. Azim nudged her closer so their hips bumped and she let out a gasp of shock. Malik had not touched her once, save for a formal hand-shake. This felt like tangling with electricity.

'You don't…?' Azim prompted, tilting her chin up with his other hand so she was forced to meet his eyes. They were as black as ever, yet somehow they no longer seemed menacing or cruel. She felt as if she could lose herself in them, in him. Fall into their dark depths and never come out. 'Or you do?'

She had no idea what to say, and so she simply shook her head helplessly, parted her lips although no words emerged. Azim laughed softly.

'You are sending out mixed signals, Johara,' he breathed as his fingertips trailed sparks up the side of her face, a tiny, tingling caress. 'I think you are scared, but I think you also want me to kiss you.'

Kiss. She'd never even come close to being kissed. Yet now her gaze dropped of its own accord to Azim's mouth, those full, mobile lips that she'd noticed that morning. Lips that were coming closer to hers, and made her heart race. She did want to kiss him. She didn't understand it, and a distant, panicky part of her brain insisted she didn't really want that, she couldn't possibly, but her body was saying otherwise. Her body was clamouring for Azim to close the mere inch between their mouths so she could feel the taste and touch of him on her lips.

And then she did. Azim brushed a kiss over her lips, as soft as a whisper, so Johara was left wondering if it had really happened. And then another brush that made her whole body tense like a violin that had experienced the first swipe of a bow across its strings, before his mouth settled firmly on hers and a symphony of sensation began.

She felt as if fireworks were popping in her mind, all over her body, as Azim explored the soft contours of her mouth with gentle assurance, fitting her body close to his, hips bumping, breasts pressed against the hard wall of his chest. Her hands tangled in his hair as her head fell back and he sweetly plundered her mouth.

She had had no idea that kissing felt like this. Could be this...*wonderful.* Her body was tingling, pleasure zinging through her like bubbles in champagne. She barely knew what she was doing, only that she desperately wanted more. Her hands drifted from his hair to his face, her fingertips trailing down his cheek and then brushing the raised, puckered flesh of his scar.

Azim stilled for a second and then broke the kiss. Johara blinked up at him, her lips swollen, her mind reeling. Azim gazed down at her, his expression as inscrutable and unchanged as ever, save for a faint flush on his sharp cheekbones, a hint of smug triumph in his dark eyes.

'That was a good start,' he said, and moved away from her. Johara simply stared. She didn't know what had happened, or why. That kiss, with its passion and promise, was the last thing she'd expected. No, she acknowledged with a plunging realisation, her *response* was the last thing she'd expected.

Azim had short-circuited her senses, utterly overwhelmed them. She'd never felt that blaze of desire streaking through her body before, lighting everything up, burning away common sense or rational thought. For those few blissful moments it had taken over everything, made her act like someone she couldn't recognise, didn't even know.

'Do you make a habit of kissing people like that?' she asked shakily.

'No,' Azim answered. 'Only my bride.'

'I'm not your bride yet.'

'No,' he agreed, 'but you will be.' He paused, turning back to level her with a single, assured look. 'Today.'

For a second Johara, her mind still spinning from Azim's kiss, couldn't make sense of the words. Finally her brain kicked into belated gear. 'What do you mean, *today*?'

'Exactly that. I have arranged a civil service at a courthouse nearby.' He spoke matter-of-factly, as if this were an everyday occurrence. 'We're expected there in a little over an hour.'

'An hour?' Johara goggled. 'You expect me to marry you in an *hour*?'

Azim's stare was flat and uncompromising. 'Yes, that is my expectation, and it is yours as well.'

'But…' Her mouth was dry, her heart pounding. *And she'd thought one week was fast.* 'What about my parents? And your people?'

'They are your people too, Johara.'

That might have been so, but they didn't feel like her people. Alazar was a strange country, a place she went to on rare occasions to play-act at being a sultana-in-waiting for her father's sake. And Azim, no matter how he'd just kissed her, was still a strange man. She wasn't ready to marry him. She wasn't ready emotionally and as for *physically*—

Her insides lurched like a ship in a gale. Was he expecting a wedding night along with the wedding? Images, blurred by ignorance and yet shockingly specific in parts, danced through her mind. Candlelight on burnished skin. Limbs twined among satin sheets. Kisses like the one she'd experienced, but even more explosive. And yet *marriage*, in a matter of minutes.

'Why?' she asked, the word bursting out of her like a bullet from a gun, reverberating through the room, shattering the taut stillness. 'Why are you rushing things? Don't you want a proper wedding, a real ceremony, back in Alazar?' She snatched a trump card and threw it down. 'Don't your people?'

'Yes, and they will get one. This is but a civil service. In five days the wedding ceremony, a religious occasion, will still go ahead. But make no mistake,' he finished, a warning glint in his eyes. 'The ceremony today will be valid.'

Johara stared at him, caught between despondency, fear and a new, dangerous excitement she didn't want to examine too closely. 'I'm not ready,' she said, even though she knew Azim wouldn't care.

'I can't trust you not to run away again,' he answered flatly. 'Not that you'll have much opportunity.'

'If I promise…?'

'I don't trust your promises,' he returned. 'And I will not change my mind.'

A last bid, desperate, pathetic. 'Does my father know you're doing this—?'

'Yes,' Azim said, and it was the flicker of pity in his eyes that sealed her fate. Made her realise how hopeless it all was. 'He does.'

So her father had no objection to Azim spiriting her away and essentially forcing her to the altar. Of course not.

She couldn't escape marriage. If she ran away, Azim would find her again. And even if he didn't, she wasn't at all sure she could survive on her own. She hadn't done a great job of it in her few hours of freedom.

Besides, she acknowledged bleakly, what about her duty and honour? They were concepts she still believed in even if her father had flung them at her like insults. Perhaps as the wife of the Sultan she could carve out a life for herself, do good in the world. Certainly she'd have more opportunity for it than a life on the run, penniless and destitute.

And maybe Azim's lack of interest could be a good thing. *Love is a facile emotion.* At least she would have no reason to go chasing after it, and be hurt again, the way her father had hurt her.

She'd made a desperate, childish bid for freedom, but now she needed to grow up and face her future. She would not shirk her responsibility simply because her father had not been the man she'd thought he was. The realisation was like swallowing lead. It rested in the pit of her stomach, heavy and poisonous.

'It won't be all bad,' Azim said, and Johara let out a huff of despairing laughter.

'Is that supposed to make me feel better?'

'Why shouldn't it? You look,' he informed her with a

touch of acid, 'as if you are about to head to the gallows. I'm simply reminding you that becoming the queen of a country and enjoying a life of luxury and means is hardly a prison sentence.'

'No,' Johara agreed, because he was making her sound rather spoiled, 'but it is a life sentence.'

Something flashed in his eyes and she had the bizarre sense that she'd hurt him with her words. It hardly seemed possible, and before she could process whatever that flash had been he'd turned away.

'Yes,' he agreed tonelessly. 'It is that. Now I suggest you go and prepare for your wedding day.'

CHAPTER FIVE

AZIM SPARED A sideways glance for his new bride, noting her pale face and downcast gaze as she slid into the limousine. She'd been silent since he'd told her to prepare for their wedding day, offering only monosyllabic answers to the few attempts at conversation he'd made, and saying even less during their brief wedding ceremony.

She had looked lovely, if subdued, in a pale pink dress with an overlay of pearl-encrusted gauze, her heavy, dark hair pulled back in a low chignon. Azim had instructed a nearby boutique to send several appropriate gowns to his flat, and he'd been gratified that Johara had chosen one.

A few days ago he'd told himself he hadn't cared what Johara thought, that her opinion didn't matter. Now he realised it *had* to matter, at least for now, because constant hostility was simply too aggravating to deal with. Of course, once they were in Alazar he would simply send her to the harem and see her only as required. That had always been his plan, but now, glancing at her subdued profile, he felt a twinge of...what? Not quite regret. But something, an emotion he wasn't used to, and one that did not feel comfortable. Pain twanged through his head and he leaned back against the seat and closed his eyes, taking a deep, even breath. He could not afford to have a migraine now.

'Are you all right?' Johara asked quietly and Azim cracked open an eye.

'I'm fine.'

Her soft grey gaze moved over him, without rancour or bitterness, which pierced him in a bittersweet way, like a honey-tipped arrow finding a crack to slide through. 'It's only that you looked as if you were in pain.'

Azim tensed against another laser-strike in his head. 'I'm fine,' he repeated more firmly and closed his eyes again. Johara let out a soft sigh.

He had no idea what she was thinking. He realised he was curious, and that annoyed him further. He hadn't meant to get involved. He didn't get involved with anyone. He'd long ago learned the hard lesson of trust and when it was misplaced—*always*.

No, trust was most certainly not going to be part of his relationship with Johara. In fact, relationship was the wrong word entirely. They had an arrangement, nothing more, and he really didn't care what she thought—about anything.

'I don't even know where we're going,' Johara said. 'Are we flying back to Alazar today?'

'No, we are going to Italy. I have business in Naples.'

'Business…?' She turned to him, eyes wide with curiosity. 'What kind of business?'

'I need to review the accounts of my company before I return to Alazar.' As reluctant as he was to hand over that responsibility, he knew he needed to. He had to focus on his country now. His crown.

'I didn't know you had your own company. What is it?'

'A real estate company. Olivieri Holdings.'

Her brow creased. 'Olivieri…?'

'I went by the name Rafael Olivieri before I remembered who I was.' And Rafael Olivieri was dead now. Dead and buried, at last, with all of his shame.

'That must have felt so strange.' Her features softened and Azim looked away.

'It was what it was.'

'What about the people who knew you as Rafael? The life you left behind?'

He tensed, his gaze remaining on the window as Paris traffic streamed by. Memories came, unbidden, of those years of hard work and fruitless fighting. Fury and shame. Pain and then finally, sweetly, so sweetly—revenge. Ruining the man who had ruined him still hadn't felt like enough. It didn't make up for all the wasted years. Only claiming his inheritance, his destiny, would do that. 'What about it?' he asked tonelessly.

'Don't you miss it? Them?'

He slid his phone out of his pocket and began to scroll through messages. 'No.' There wasn't a single person he missed from his old life. Not one. Enemies, employees and meaningless liaisons. He'd easily turned his back on them all. Twenty years of striving and success reduced to nothing.

Everything had been centred on gaining his revenge against Paolo Caivano—and when he'd done that he'd re-alised it hadn't been enough. It was only when he'd seen his grandfather on the news, when he'd remembered about Alazar, that he'd realised what he needed to do. What would make up for all he'd endured.

Johara was silent for a few minutes and Azim thumbed a few buttons on his phone, answering some quick emails.

'How long will we stay in Naples?' she finally asked.

'A few days.' He glanced up, giving her a cool smile of intent. 'We need to be in Alazar this weekend for our proper wedding.'

Azim kept himself immersed in work on the short flight to Naples, and then for the drive to his villa on the city's outskirts. Johara hadn't attempted to engage him in conversation, and Azim had told himself he preferred it, although he'd been unsettlingly aware of her presence next to him, every draw and sigh of her breathing, the subtle vanilla and almond scent that wafted towards him whenever she moved. Her hair was so dark it almost had a deep blue sheen, and it made Azim wonder how soft it felt. He hadn't got as much work done as he would have wished, the realisation of what a distraction his bride was a further aggravation.

By the time they arrived at his villa Johara looked pale and drawn. She didn't say anything as she stepped into the house, glancing around at the luxurious furnishings, the soaring ceilings and marble floors, the French windows open to the terrace bathed in twilight.

His butler, Antonio, hurried forward to take their bags, and Johara gave the man a genuine smile that made Azim realise she had never smiled at him like that. He felt annoyed for noticing—and caring.

She stood in the centre of the foyer, a solitary figure, her eyes luminous, her hair dark against her pale face, her slender body swathed in pink. In spite of every determination to remain unattached, Azim found he was strangely moved by the sight.

'We should eat. I rang ahead for my chef to prepare something.'

'Oh.' Johara turned, seeming startled by this simple act of practical kindness. 'That would be nice.'

Azim nodded tersely, feeling as uncomfortable as she obviously was. Neither of them knew the protocol. It would be easier simply to leave her, busy himself with work as he had done for the last few hours, but for some absurd reason he was reluctant to do so. She looked so nervous, so fragile, and he wanted to do something about it. The trouble was, he just didn't know what. He was not a gentle man. He was not accustomed to kindness. Everything about this situation felt strange, and yet he still could not keep from wanting to soften the blow for his new bride, or at least the landing.

Johara looked around the foyer, her glazed eyes barely taking in all the luxurious details. Her body was buzzing with nervous energy, her mind a spinning maelstrom of both anxiety and expectation.

Everything had happened so *quickly*—she'd felt as if she'd been watching a film of someone else's life rather than taking part in the major action of her own. She was *married*. How had that happened? And more importantly, what happened now?

She had no idea what to expect. Oh, she knew the logistics of a wedding night—she wasn't *that* innocent. But as for Azim…there had been moments, unexpected and startling, when he'd almost seemed kind. He'd ordered several gorgeous dresses for her to wear for the ceremony, and at times he'd seemed concerned for her, his forehead furrowed as he glanced at her, dark eyes sweeping over her as if checking for injuries. And of course there had been that kiss…

But maybe that kiss hadn't been kind. Perhaps it had simply been a display of the power he had over her, the power he intended to wield, maybe even tonight.

'The food will be ready shortly.'

Johara turned to see Azim standing in the doorway of the enormous sitting room she'd wandered into, his expression as grim as ever. Was he expecting to consummate their marriage tonight? She couldn't bring herself to ask.

'That's good,' she managed, struggling to find even the simplest words. 'Thank you.'

He nodded towards her dress. 'Would you like to change?'

Into what? Johara glanced down at the lovely dress she'd worn for the wedding. It had made her feel beautiful, with its gauzy, pearl-encrusted fabric swishing gently about her legs. It was one of the prettiest things she'd ever worn, and she'd been touched that Azim had thought to provide it for her. Stupidly touched, perhaps. As with her father, it had cost him nothing, or at least very little. It didn't *mean* anything.

'I thought you might be more comfortable in something else,' Azim explained when she didn't reply. 'There are clothes upstairs. I had them sent from several boutiques. They will provide a wardrobe for you until we return to Alazar.'

Johara couldn't tell if this was another one of his autocratic commands or an act of kind consideration. Maybe both. 'All right, thank you.'

'I'll show you.'

She followed him up the sweeping staircase to a bedroom decorated in shades of cream and gold, everything sumptuous, at least a dozen pillows of silk and satin piled high on the king-sized bed.

Glancing at that huge bed, she couldn't keep from imagining it occupied, and a sudden, shocking image of naked bodies twined and flickering with candlelight burst into her brain...where had *that* fantasy come from? Their wedding night wasn't about fantasy. It was about expediency. Even so all the oxygen seemed to have been sucked from the air, and she felt light-headed and dizzy.

'The clothes are in the dressing room.' Azim gestured to an adjoining room that looked to be nearly as large as the bedroom.

'Thank you.' Johara could feel her skin heat with embarrassment. Had Azim seen something of what she'd been thinking in her eyes, her face? His expression was as inscrutable as ever.

'I'll be downstairs. You may join me in the dining room when you are ready.'

'All right—'

He left the room without waiting for her reply, and Johara let out the breath she'd been holding. Every exchange they'd had had been punctuated by abrupt stops and sudden silences, so Johara felt as if they were jolting along, her psyche forced to absorb every juddering bump. She wondered if talking to this man, her *husband*, would ever seem natural. Would they ever chat or laugh together? Share anything other than a bed? Or would it be better, safer, for her not to want those things? Even if they didn't love each other, she reflected, she hoped they could get along. Enmity was exhausting, especially when it was coupled with enforced intimacy.

She eyed the king-sized bed again in front of her with a shiver of apprehension and then went into the dressing room, stopping in amazement at the sight of at least a dozen dresses hanging in the huge wardrobe, and tops and trousers, as well as a host of gauzy, silky underthings, folded in the drawers. A wardrobe, indeed. There were more clothes in there than she'd ever had in her life. She could hardly believe that Azim had bought her so many things. How did he even know her size? Her *bra* size?

It was thoughtful and yet at the same time it wasn't. Was she never going to be able to choose her own clothes, or anything, ever again? Was Azim going to dictate everything about her life? So far he seemed to expect to, and the thought of fighting, no doubt uselessly, over every little thing made Johara want to both weep and sag in exhaustion.

And what was she supposed to pick to wear? One of the cocktail dresses? Or a silky negligee? Letting out a groan of frustration, she finally settled on a pair of flowing palazzo pants in soft jersey and a matching loose top in aquamarine. Then, taking a deep breath, she headed down to the dining room.

Azim was standing by the window, his back to her, when she came in. He turned as he heard her, his eyes flaring as he took in her appearance, his gaze moving slowly over her, leaving a warm ripple of awareness in its wake. She felt suddenly, achingly conscious of the smooth jersey sliding over her skin, the peaks of her breasts and the heat between her thighs. How did he create such a reaction in her by just a look? It scared her, how her body responded to him even when her mind was trying to maintain a cool distance. She wasn't ready for this. She had no experience, nothing to give her some perspective or simply some calm.

'That smells good.' She nodded towards the table laden with dishes, still conscious of Azim's presence, feeling his gaze like a brand on her skin. Blindly she surveyed the table, barely taking in the different options.

'What would you like?' Azim asked, his shoulder brushing her breast as he reached for a plate. Johara had to suppress the urge to shiver.

'I…I don't know.' Her voice came out in a humiliating, hoarse stammer.

'You can relax,' Azim told her as he began to fill up the plate with a variety of succulent dishes—a risotto with vegetables, pasta with ragu sauce, stuffed peppers. It all looked mouth-watering and yet with the way her stomach was churning Johara didn't know if she'd be able to eat a single mouthful.

She let out a shaky, uncertain laugh. 'Can I?'

'I'm not going to ravish you over the dining room table,'

Azim informed her flatly. 'Or even tonight at all. Our wedding night will happen after our wedding in Alazar.'

'Oh…well…' She had no idea what to say. The flood of relief she felt was mingled with an unsettling trickle of disappointment.

'Relieved?' Azim's voice rang with the sharp note of cynicism. 'I can assure you, when it comes time to consummate our marriage, you'll be as eager for it as I will.'

That arrogant statement felt like both a promise and a threat, and it brought a flush to her cheeks and a skip to her heartbeat. She still didn't know whether to be thrilled or terrified by the prospect. 'Why wait, then?' she dared to ask, then wished she hadn't. She'd sounded as if she was disappointed in the delay, and she wasn't. She couldn't be.

'Because our people will be waiting to see a sign that you're a virgin,' Azim stated baldly. 'And if we cannot provide it, we will both be shamed.'

'Really?' Johara blinked. 'That seems a bit…archaic.'

He shrugged. 'It is the reality.' His smile was twisted as he added, 'But at least you have a few days' reprieve.' He nodded towards the open French doors, the gauzy curtains billowing in the evening breeze. 'We will eat out on the terrace.'

'All right.' Although the reason for it was practically medieval, the reprieve, Johara realised, was needed. The fact that she now had at least a few days to unwind made the tension unknot in her shoulders, and gave her the confidence to suggest, 'Maybe then we could…talk.'

'Talk?' He sounded both surprised and appalled by the suggestion. 'About what?'

'About ourselves. Since we're married, shouldn't we get to know one another?' Azim stared at her blankly and Johara remembered that he had already informed her he didn't want to get to know her. He knew everything he needed to already. The look on his face reminded her of that all too well; he looked completely nonplussed by the suggestion, as if she'd suggested something both outrageous and pointless. 'Never mind,' she muttered, feeling stupid, and she took her full plate and headed out to the terrace, the cool breeze and stunning view of the surrounding hills cloaked in violet restoring her spirits only a little.

How on earth was she going to make this marriage work? She picked at her salad, her appetite receding. She was by nature optimistic; she'd made herself be, after living with her mother's endless sadness for so long. She'd always chosen to see the bright side, to choose a smile over a frown. But right now she had a glimmer of understanding of the despondency her mother had felt, the years yawning in front of her, barren and hopeless. Azim didn't want to know her. He didn't want any kind of relationship. He simply wanted her as his bride—and in his bed.

'What exactly do you want to talk about?' Azim stood in the doorway, a plate balanced in one hand, his expression drawn in lines of taut resignation.

'It's not meant to be some form of torture,' Johara answered tartly.

'I am not used to talking about myself.' Azim sat down across from her at the small wrought-iron table and squinted at the horizon. His profile reminded Johara of the bust of a Roman consul or emperor, the smooth curve of his skull, the patrician nose, the strong jaw. The only blemish to the perfection of his face was the scar snaking its way down one cheek. Johara wondered how he'd got it, and knew she wouldn't ask. Not yet anyway, and at this rate probably not ever. 'In fact,' Azim continued without looking at her, 'I am not used to making much conversation at all.'

That, at least, was something. 'Why not?' Johara asked.

He shrugged powerful shoulders, muscles rippling. 'As a child it was not encouraged. And then...' He stopped, as if he'd said all she needed to know.

Johara's stomach turned over. She was afraid to probe too much, afraid of Azim's sudden anger or stinging set-downs, and yet she was intensely curious. This man was her husband now. She wanted to understand him. She wanted to have some kind of relationship, *any* kind, even if he didn't. 'Do you mean after you were kidnapped...?' A terse nod was all the confirmation she got and even though he was clearly discouraging her from continuing, she made herself ask, 'You said you remembered some things...?'

'I do not remember the kidnapping.' His voice was flat, his shuttered gaze still on the horizon. 'All I remember is waking up in a hospital bed in Italy, not knowing who I was or what had happened.'

'That sounds awful.' He'd only been fourteen, a mere boy. She could not even imagine enduring such a thing. 'But someone must have taken care of you, since you were only a boy. And you had your company eventually...' Azim did not reply, and Johara shook her head slowly, absorbing the enormity of the seismic shifts he'd experienced in his life. 'Where were you for all that time? Who was taking care of you?'

He smiled slightly at that, a bitter twisting of his lips that drew at his scar. 'No one.'

'But you were only fourteen. Someone must have been... I mean, what were you doing?'

His gaze had turned even more distant, focused inward, making him seem more inscrutable and inaccessible than ever. 'Surviving,' he finally said, and there was a terrible bleakness in his voice that made Johara ache even though she didn't understand why.

* * *

Why did people talk about themselves? It was torture, like peeling back a layer of skin, exposing the raw nerves to air and sunlight. He didn't want to tell Johara anything about his past. He didn't want to have that kind of relationship with her; he didn't want her to have that kind of knowledge and power over him. And yet in just a few short sentences he'd told her more than he'd told anyone else.

Surviving. And sometimes barely, at that. It was just a word, and yet from the way her lush mouth turned down, her eyes crinkling at the corners, he knew he'd said too much. She pitied him, and he couldn't stand the notion. He'd been pitied before, and, worse, he'd *deserved* to be pitied. He hated the thought of enduring such a thing again. He shouldn't have said anything at all.

'What about you? How have you filled your time in the south of France?' He imagined a life of leisure, lounging by the pool, attending endless parties. Johara was innocent, but that didn't mean she was unspoiled.

'I've lived a very quiet life. I helped my mother, and I gardened.' She shrugged, smiling. 'Not very interesting.'

'You must have gone out to parties and things.'

'No. My mother is often unwell and so we lived just the two of us, very quietly. I went to the village sometimes, and I had a tutor for a few years, and of course my garden to keep me company.'

It was not the life he'd expected her to have. 'What about friends?'

'I don't really have any friends.' She shrugged, her smile philosophical and yet touched with sadness. 'Some of our staff. Lucille, the cook, and her husband, Thomas. I'll miss them.'

'And yet this was the life you were desperate to maintain?' He heard a note of contempt creep into his voice, and saw Johara flinch. Still he could not keep himself from continuing. 'This was what you were running away from me for? A garden and a sick mother, with only the cook as your friend?'

Johara lifted her chin, her slender shoulders straightening. 'No. I was running away from you because I wanted my freedom to choose to live as I wanted. To decide my own destiny.'

'Even I do not have that freedom.'

She frowned. 'What do you mean?'

'It is both my duty and destiny to be the next Sultan. To shirk it would be unconscionable.'

'And yet you still have a choice.'

A choice? No. The Sultanate was more than a birthright; it was a necessity. To validate who he was and what had happened to him, all he'd endured. Sometimes it felt like the only way he could save his soul, if indeed that was a possibility at all. 'You had a choice as well,' Azim pointed out. 'You said the vows of your own accord, Johara. If you'd really wanted out of this marriage, you could have told the judge you were being coerced.'

She flushed and looked away. Azim wondered why he was pressing the point. He'd been intending to use this time together as a way to help her to relax, and instead he was practically picking a fight. Aggression was more familiar to him, keeping in control a necessity he could not relinquish. Johara's innocent questions had touched him too rawly, made him feel too unsure. And the truth was he wanted to know. 'Why didn't you, at that?' he demanded. 'A word to the judge…it could have been simple.' Although not that simple, considering he'd paid the judge beforehand to keep things straightforward. But she hadn't known that.

Johara's face remained averted. 'Because it seemed

pointless,' she answered quietly. 'As well as dishonour-able. Like you I have a duty. I have been told it my whole life. To walk away from it…and for what? A chance to really screw up my life, to live in poverty or worse?' She wrinkled her nose. 'This seemed like the lesser evil.'

'Is that supposed to make me feel better?' he asked, parroting her own question from earlier.

'No, not really. You asked me, and I answered honestly.' She took a deep breath and met his gaze unflinchingly, her eyes shining like silver with courage and determination. 'But now that we are married, I would like to get along with you, Azim. I would like to get to know you. I would like us to be…friends, at least.'

'Friends?' He repeated the word disbelievingly, every-thing inside him resisting such a suggestion. He didn't have *friends*.

'Why shouldn't we?' Johara pressed. 'We're married. We're going to share our lives together, have children one day, God willing. Wouldn't it be better for both of us if we could actually like each other a little bit? Share with each other our concerns, our fears, our hopes…?'

Azim stared at her in appalled amazement. Johara's view of marriage was entirely at odds with his own. He had no intention of sharing those things with anyone, of giving anyone that kind of power over him, exposing him-self to scrutiny and judgement.

And yet…for a second, he could almost picture how it could be. He thought of his brother Malik, who had found that kind of relationship with his fiancée, Gracie. He imag-ined himself as Malik now was with Gracie, smiling, re-laxed, easily affectionate. *Weak*.

He was not his brother. He couldn't be that man. His life experience had hardened him, ossified any natural craving for such closeness. Despite that one treacherous flicker of yearning, the possibility horrified him. He could not seek it now, and he did not want to.

'We are not friends,' he stated flatly. 'We are husband and wife. I told you what I needed from you,' he reminded her, ignoring the hurt look on her face as he continued relentlessly, 'And that is all I want.'

CHAPTER SIX

BY THE TIME Johara woke the next morning Azim had already left for work. She hadn't seen him after dinner; Azim had closeted himself in his study and then they'd retired to separate bedrooms. She spent the morning wandering aimlessly around the large, elegant rooms of the villa; none of them possessed a single personal memento or photograph, nothing to give her a better idea of who her husband was. Yet according to the butler, Antonio, who had warmed up to her after the first few taciturn hours, this was Azim's main residence.

It looked, Johara thought, as if every sign of individuality or interest had been removed, scrubbed away, but perhaps it hadn't been there to begin with. It was as if, in having amnesia for twenty years, Azim had simply not existed for all that time. Where were his friends, his memories, his pictures and keepsakes? Books, even? There wasn't a single one in the house beyond some hand-tooled leather volumes that looked as if they'd never been opened.

Perhaps he kept his more personal items in a private room, his bedroom or study. She didn't dare look for such a room, not with the staff seeming to watch her every move. In the end Johara retreated to the gardens, vast and ruthlessly landscaped, simply for some privacy from the stultifying silence and watching eyes.

The sun was hot on her head, the sky a deep, pure blue, but Johara took little pleasure in her surroundings. She wanted to get to know her husband, at least a little; she wanted to find some chink in his inscrutable armour, some glimpse into the mind and maybe even the heart of this man she had just pledged to spend all her days with. She didn't want to spend the rest of her life with a stranger.

She wasn't looking for love or even much affection. She'd learned the dangers of believing someone loved you, hoping for it, trusting it. No, she wasn't about to go down that route again. But why couldn't they be friends?

Johara thought she could be patient, if she felt it was simply a matter of time for Azim and her to get to know one another. But she feared with a leaden and growing certainty that it wasn't. She would never get to know Azim, because he did not want to be known. He had locked himself like a vault, and he had no intention of giving Johara, or anyone, the key.

From the French doors Antonio called her for lunch, and with a sigh Johara rose from the bench. She ate alone at a table that seated twenty, working her way through three courses and wondering if this was what the rest of her life was going to look like.

It wasn't as if she even cared for Azim, she told herself. She knew she didn't. She barely knew the man, after all, and what she knew she wasn't sure she particularly liked. And yet she *wanted* to know him. She was married, and yet she felt more isolated than ever, and that felt wrong.

After lunch she plucked up the courage to go out. She got her coat and her bag and asked Antonio to fetch the driver.

'But…*signora* is not going out?' Antonio asked, his forehead creased with concern.

'I thought I'd see some of Naples's sights.' Whatever those were.

Antonio was looking troubled, shaking his head, and Johara kept her sunny smile with effort.

'Perhaps you can recommend…?' she began, only to have Antonio shake his head more vigorously.

'No, no, I am sorry, *signora*. The *signor* does not permit you to leave the estate.'

Her heart started a slow, steady descent towards her toes. 'Even with the driver…?'

Antonio looked regretful but very firm. 'I am sorry, but no.'

Johara stared at him, feeling frustrated and, worse, humiliated. So she really was a prisoner. Did Azim really think she was going to make a run for it, now that they were wed? She accepted that he had little reason to trust her, but her enforced imprisonment still rankled. She supposed it would only be worse in Alazar, when she was banished to the palace's harem, only to be brought out like a trophy.

Holding her head high with effort, she left Antonio and retreated again to the garden. She'd always taken solace in nature, but the manicured hedges and sterile-looking flowers were far from the wild and unruly garden she'd cultivated back in Provence. Quite suddenly, she missed her home with a ferocity that left her breathless and winded. She wanted her garden, her stillroom with its stoppered bottles and jars, the kitchen with sunbeams slanting on the floor and Lucille humming tunelessly as she cooked.

She wanted her big grey cat, Gavroche, and her favourite books, and the freedom that her life, small and simple as it had been, had possessed. She even missed her mother, who had been nothing but a sullen, silent presence for years, hardly ever coming out of her bedroom. Anything but this—this loneliness and isolation, wandering around empty rooms with no company, no purpose.

She'd been married but one day and she was already regretting it. Deeply. Johara sank onto a garden bench under a cypress tree and closed her eyes. This time there was no escape.

Azim scrolled through the latest accounts in his office in downtown Naples, barely able to keep his mind on the columns of figures on his screen. He had important business to attend to, checking the accounts of his real estate interests in Italy before returning to Alazar, and he couldn't concentrate for more than a few minutes at a time. He kept thinking of Johara, wondering what she was doing. Thinking. *Feeling*, which was extraordinarily aggravating, because he wasn't like that. His marriage wasn't like that. Yet for some reason he kept picturing her in his mind's eye as she'd been after their wedding, looking solitary and lonely, her slender body encased in pink, her dark, heavy hair pulled back, a few tendrils framing a face that held such an expression of sorrow and resignation he was torn between regret and frustration. He knew how she felt. He understood that kind of loneliness and desperation, the resignation to a fate you never, ever would have chosen.

And yet…her marriage to him did not have to be such a *wake*. Nobody had died. And he knew what real suffering looked like, felt like. It wasn't this.

Even so she stayed in his thoughts, and sometimes he felt as if he could almost catch a whiff of her vanilla and almond scent, which was ridiculous.

By four o'clock he gave up on the day's work, knowing he was too distracted. Impatiently he pressed the intercom on his phone. 'Send Signor Andretti here to discuss the last month's accounts.' He'd hand everything over to Andretti, something he wouldn't normally do, and go home. See what Johara was up to. Hell, maybe he'd even talk to her, the way she'd wanted him to last night.

While that prospect of her getting to know him still had his insides shrinking in horror, he wondered if perhaps *he* could get to know *her*.

He had too many secrets, too many darknesses, to reveal them to Johara. If he'd disgusted her already, what on earth would she think when she learned just how low he'd been brought? How low he'd stooped? The idea of anyone, but especially his wife, learning his weaknesses made him tense with horror. He would never give someone that kind of insight or power. Never again.

But he could ask her questions. Learn more about his bride, and then perhaps when his curiosity—and lust— were satisfied, he could concentrate on the far more pressing business of securing his throne.

An hour later he left the office for the sprawling villa on the outskirts of Naples. He quickened his step, scanning the marble foyer for a sight of his bride, half-expecting her to be waiting for him there.

'Where is Signora Bahjat?' he demanded of Antonio, his butler.

'She is out, *signor,*' the man replied with a short bow.

'Out?' Azim stared at him in disbelief. Had Johara defied him even in this? And what about his staff? 'Out where? I gave strict instructions that she was to stay in the villa.'

'Only—only out to the garden,' the old man stammered, clearly alarmed by Azim's ferocious expression. 'She has been sitting out there for hours.'

'She has?' Azim frowned, not liking that for some reason. 'I'll go find her now.'

Too late he realised how that sounded, as if he were so

besotted by his bride that he had to see her the moment he came through the door. He decided he didn't care.

He strode through the palatial rooms of the villa, all of them gorgeously decorated and glaringly empty. He felt a tightening in his midsection, an anxiety he didn't understand.

He threw open the French doors that led to the garden, breathing in the scents of jasmine and oleander. The sun was just starting its descent, bathing the terraced gardens in golden light, the sky turning to violet, the colour of a bruise. He surveyed the expanse of lawn, the landscaped shrubs and carefully tended flowerbeds, but he didn't see Johara. His anxiety increased. He had top-notch security on his estate, out of necessity. Paolo Caivano, broken as he was, still wanted revenge, and always would, as long as Azim was alive. And he wanted his villa back.

Azim's mouth curved in a cold smile as he thought about how unlikely that was. He'd utterly destroyed his one-time tormentor, at least financially. Still, the man had friends in ugly places.

Slowly he strolled through the gardens, his gaze narrowed as he looked for Johara. He didn't actually think Caivano could have got to her, but the possibility was enough to make his muscles clench. Maybe he'd forbid her from coming outside.

Then he saw her, sitting on a wrought-iron garden bench under a cypress tree. She looked peaceful, her head resting against the trunk of the tree, her eyes closed, a slight smile on her face. The sight of her made something in Azim twist painfully, a sensation he didn't particularly like.

'What have you been doing out here for so long?' His voice grated on his own ears, harsh and demanding, too much, and definitely not the tone he'd meant to take. But he'd been *worried*. She didn't realise the dangers the way he did. She didn't understand how much was at stake.

Johara opened her eyes, the instinctive smile that had started to bloom across her face sliding off as she caught sight of his expression, registered his tone. 'I was simply enjoying the garden,' she informed him stiffly. 'Is that a crime?'

'Antonio said you've been out here for hours.'

She lifted her chin. 'So?'

This was not going to plan at all, Azim realised with frustration. He was making a mess of what he'd intended to be a friendly conversation. He tried again. 'Why?' It came out sounding like an interrogation.

Johara's gaze narrowed. 'Because I enjoy being out of doors, and I was bored inside. The comforts of your home only last so long, and, as I was forbidden from venturing outside the estate, I decided to come out here.' Her voice was touched with acid and Azim drew back, needled.

'You know why those measures are in place.' Although her running away wasn't the real reason, at least not the main one. She would be foolish to try to flee from him here in Naples, and in any case he knew she wouldn't get very far.

'I'm married to you now. What's the point of my running away? In any case I've already accepted my life sentence.' She leaned her head back against the seat and closed her eyes, effectively dismissing him.

Azim stared at her, silently fuming. He'd come out here to talk to her, to do what she'd been wanting him to do and get to know her. What a waste of time that had been. They'd only ended up trading accusations and insults.

'Don't go out to the garden any more,' he said abruptly.

Her eyes opened, anger sparking in their silvery depths. 'You're forbidding me from spending time outside? In a walled garden with security cameras all over the place? What do you think is going to happen?'

A muscle ticced in his jaw, and he felt the first flickers of a headache at his temples. He knew he was being over-bearing and unreasonable, but he'd been pushed into it by her insouciant indifference.

'I am speaking for your safety,' he bit out.

'How thoughtful of you,' she drawled. 'Because it seems like you're simply trying to show me your power. Again.'

'I have enemies in this city,' Azim said, the words drawn from him with terse reluctance. Johara's eyes widened in surprised alarm.

'Enemies? What kind of enemies?'

He shrugged, having no intention of giving her any of the grim details. 'Power and wealth breed envy and malice,' he answered repressively. 'That is all you need to know.'

'Am I really in danger?' Her tongue darted out and touched her lips, causing an entirely inappropriate arrow of lust to dart through him. Their wedding night could not come soon enough. That, at least, he hoped would be simple.

'I don't know,' he admitted gruffly. He didn't know what Caivano was capable of anymore, or how much power he had, if any, but he certainly didn't intend to take chances. In the many years since he'd escaped the man, he'd always watched his back. Hired bodyguards and taken bullet-proof cars—but that was no more than what many Neopolitan businessmen did these days. 'I'm not willing to take the risk. Any risk.'

'So I have to stay in the villa all the time?' Johara said. 'And not even go out to the garden?'

'We're only here for a few days.'

She glanced at the walls topped with barbed wire, her

scornful gaze taking in the many security cameras, and Azim knew she was doubting the truth of what he said. Hell, so was he. His estate was safe. He knew that much. He'd been foolish to restrict her so much, but he'd been piqued by her seeming indifference. This, he supposed, was why he did not attempt relationships of any kind. This and a lot of other reasons.

'Fine,' Johara said as she rose from the bench, a lovely vision of wounded dignity. 'I don't mind. These are the most boring, soulless gardens I've ever seen.'

And with that last insult she turned and strode back to the villa, her cheeks bright with angry colour, her head held high.

No matter how much she tried, how much she pretended, Johara knew she couldn't escape the truth. This place was a prison. Her *life* was a prison, and her new husband seemed intent on proving it to her again and again.

The stupid thing was, she'd actually been looking forward to him coming home. To seeing him again. She'd hoped they might talk again, at least a little. They'd share a meal, figure out some kind of new normal.

And then she'd seen him, and he'd been furious, punishing her to no purpose. Not being able to go out in the garden was a ridiculous restriction. The walls surrounding the estate were a foot thick and twelve feet high, with barbed wire on top. She'd counted a dozen security cameras on her stroll around the gardens. What kind of enemies did Azim have, anyway?

That, Johara realised with a chill, was a question she didn't really want to ask—or have answered. What could he have possibly done to create such enmity? It was another awful reminder that she didn't know this man, and yet she was married to him.

With her feelings in a ferment, she headed back into the villa. Its palatial rooms and sumptuous decorations left her cold; the place was as soulless as the gardens, all professionally decorated perfection without any heart or humour, or any personality. Just like its owner.

No, that wasn't fair. She was sure Azim had plenty of personality. He even, she thought, had a glimmer of humour. But heart? Just when she thought she'd found a chink in his iron armour, he behaved in a way that made Johara fear there was nothing beneath that cold exterior but more ice.

She ate dinner alone in the cavernous dining room; Antonio had informed her that Azim was working again that evening. The elderly man looked tired, stooping to serve her, and so Johara told him she could look after herself.

'But that is surely not appropriate—' Antonio protested in broken English, the only language they shared.

Johara waved a hand. 'I'm fine, Antonio, honestly. I'll go to bed soon, anyway.'

Alone in the dining room, the clink of her cutlery sounding overly loud in the spacious room, she forked a few more mouthfuls before she lost both interest and appetite. She'd spent most of her life in virtual isolation, but she had never felt as alone as this. She wasn't even sure why—in Provence she'd had the servants for company, but it wasn't all that different, really. She'd spent most of her time alone.

The difference, she supposed, was Azim. Knowing he was near and yet choosing to stay away. She'd never realised before how another person could make you feel lonely.

The restrictions he'd placed on her bothered her too—at least in Provence she'd had her garden and stillroom, the opportunity to walk into the village, experience a little bit of life. She'd had freedom, as limited as it was. Here she had nothing but the promise of long, empty days of waiting. She doubted things would change once they reached Alazar. They were more likely to get worse.

Johara pushed away from the table, determined not to give in to the despair that threatened. She couldn't think like that. She wouldn't let herself. She'd always chosen hope over despair, joy after sadness. Even when it had been hard. Even when it had hurt. Why couldn't she do the same now? Why did this feel so different, so much more?

Slowly she strolled through the spacious rooms of the villa, and then, feeling a bit as if she were venturing into Bluebeard's castle, she went upstairs and then down a shadowy corridor she thought led to Azim's bedroom. The whole villa was silent save for the occasional creak of wood or the restless slap of a shutter.

Johara walked on tiptoes, holding her breath, wondering what or who exactly she was looking for. Azim? What on earth would she say to him if she found him?

She came to the end of the corridor, and a firmly closed door she supposed led to Azim's bedroom. No light spilled from underneath it, and she could hear no sound from within. Even so she raised her hand, her closed fist hovering in front of the door to knock, yet she did not possess the courage to do it. He probably wasn't there anyway. He was most likely in a study somewhere, closeted away with business papers and his laptop.

Then she heard a sound inside the bedroom—something that almost sounded like a groan. Her whole body tensed, every muscle straining as she sought to hear more. Should she knock? Could he be hurt or ill?

The room fell silent again and Johara wavered. Azim

would be undoubtedly angry if she violated his privacy in this way. Enraged, even. But if she didn't dare to now, she never would.

Taking a deep breath, she pushed open the door.

The room was awash in shadow, the only light from the moonlight spilling through the windows. It took Johara a few moments for her eyes to adjust, and then she saw Azim sprawled in a chair by the window, his head leaning back against it, his eyes closed.

'Antonio, I told you I did not wish to be disturbed,' he said, his voice taut with suppressed pain.

'It's me.' Azim's eyes flickered open and Johara closed the door softly behind her. 'Johara.'

He closed his eyes again, his jaw clenched. 'What are you doing here?'

'You're in pain.' She moved quickly to him, her healer's instinct wanting only to help and soothe. Azim jerked away from the touch of her hand on his.

'I'm fine.' His eyes were still closed, sweat beading on his brow. He was so clearly not fine that Johara would have laughed if the situation weren't so serious, and the sight of Azim struggling against his suffering so achingly poignant.

'Is it a headache?' she asked quietly and with obvious effort he opened his eyes.

'It's nothing.'

'Why won't you tell me?' He did not reply, and Johara stared at him, her hands on her hips. He was the most insufferably stubborn man she'd ever met, arrogant and unyielding, and she wasn't even sure she liked him very much. But she didn't want to see him in pain. 'Fine. I'll be back in a moment.'

Azim's eyes fluttered closed. It only took a few moments to go to her bedroom and fetch some of the essential oils she always carried with her. Back in Azim's room she knocked softly once and then slipped inside; he hadn't moved from his chair.

Quickly she prepared a handkerchief with drops of lavender and peppermint oils. 'This should help,' she said quietly, and pressed the cloth into his hand. Azim took it without opening his eyes. His jaw was still clenched against the pain and his ashen skin looked as if it had been stretched tautly over his bones.

'What am I meant to do?' he asked after a moment, the words forced out.

'Press it to your forehead, or wherever the pain is worst.' Azim didn't move and Johara realised he was in too much pain even for that. 'Here, let me,' she said, and, kneeling in front of him, she took the cloth from his slack hand and pressed it against his temples.

'Does it hurt here?' she asked softly and Azim did not reply for a moment.

'Yes, my temples,' he finally said. 'It is always my temples.'

Gently she pressed the cloth against his head, releasing the sharp, fragrant smell of the oil. There was something startlingly intimate about the moment; she'd never been so close to a man except when Azim had kissed her. She began to massage his temples, rubbing her fingers in slow, gentle circles. Azim let out a groan.

'Does that hurt?'

'No.' A shudder went through his powerful body. 'No, it feels good.'

A dart of fierce pleasure went through her at his admission. She liked the realisation that she was helping him. It made her want something indefinable and yet more from him—what, she could not say. She continued to massage his temples, her fingers learning the feel of his skin, the ridges of bone. 'You get headaches often,' she remarked softly. She left the cloth draped across his forehead as her fingers continued to learn the shape of Azim's skull, the gentle abrasion of the stubble on his cheeks, the strong line of his jaw, moving rhythmically to relax his muscles. Every touch felt as if it brought her closer to him, an intimacy she'd never expected but now found she craved. The thought of him pushing her away now was awful. She wouldn't let him.

'Yes,' Azim admitted, the single word clearly reluctant.

'Tension makes it worse. You keep a lot of tension in your facial muscles and your jaw.' Her fingers were working their way down the side of his face, finding and unknotting the tension of muscles clenched for far too long, her thumbs brushing against his scar, the texture of it surprisingly smooth and silky. She held her breath, hoping he wouldn't pull away, everything in her singing as he relaxed into her touch.

'Probably,' Azim murmured. His voice sounded slightly slurred, his muscles loosening under her fingers. His head was back, his eyes still closed, giving Johara the freedom to study his face in leisure—the strong nose, the full lips, the surprisingly long eyelashes. The scar, which snaked its way like a river down one cheek, bisecting his face, ending right at the corner of his mouth. He was beautiful, in a hard-hewn, rugged way. Beautiful and, for the first time, accessible, at least a little.

'How long have you had the headaches?'

'Twenty years.'

The maths was easy. 'Since your kidnapping?'

He nodded, the movement barely noticeable.

'Are they caused by an injury?'

A long pause, with the only sound their breathing, the

whisper of her fingers across his skin. 'Yes. I was beaten. At least, that is assumed. I don't actually remember it.'

'Oh.' The sound was a soft gasp of sorrow. He'd said, she remembered, that he'd ended up in a hospital. 'I'm so sorry.'

'The doctors told me I'd received a concussion, which caused the amnesia. The headaches come and go.'

'But they're very painful,' Johara remarked. Things were clicking into place—the times she'd seen Azim close his eyes or clench his jaw, the way his gaze sometimes became hooded and unfocused. A sudden thought occurred to her. 'Did you have a headache at our first meeting?'

Another pause, and then he sighed, the sound long and weary. 'Yes.'

She worked her way back up to his temples, massaging in slow, rhythmic circles. She could smell his aftershave, and she was conscious of his powerful body so near to hers. She had a deep urge to press even closer, to feel the hard muscles of his chest against the softness of her own, a desire that shocked her. She was already as close to a man as she'd ever been—and yet she wanted more? 'Why didn't you tell me, then?' she asked.

'It is not something I tell anyone.' Azim hesitated before continuing, 'Pain is weakness, especially in a world leader.'

'It would have helped me to understand.'

A small, cynical smile curved his mouth, his eyes remaining closed. 'You think you would have been more predisposed to marry me if you knew I suffered from headaches?'

Johara sighed, recognising the folly of her logic. 'I don't know,' she admitted. 'But I have told you before, I want to know you. Understand you. I am your wife now, Azim.'

She wasn't prepared for the sudden electric jolt as he opened his eyes and gazed up into her face. She'd forgotten how close they were, and how fierce and dark his expression could be. 'Yes,' he agreed, his voice a low growl of sensual intent. 'You are.'

CHAPTER SEVEN

AZIM STARED UP at Johara, noting the way her pupils had dilated, her breathing turning uneven. Her breasts were brushing his chest, and had been for the last fifteen minutes, as she'd massaged his temples and face. He'd felt each point of contact with an exquisite ache, the brush of her breasts and the gentle touch of her fingers, desire warring with pain, lust with something far deeper.

He'd never experienced anything so erotic, so *emotional*, as her touching him in this way. Every brush of her fingers against his scar had jolted him with an intense emotion, made him almost want to weep even as he yearned for something he could not even name.

With her now-startled gaze fastened on his, Johara began to ease away. Azim reached out and circled her wrist with his fingers, his touch gentle but completely secure, holding her in place.

'Is the pain better?' she whispered, her tongue touching her lips and inflaming him further.

'Much.' It usually took hours for a migraine to recede, and, while the pain still lapped at his senses, it was definitely bearable. 'Thank you.'

'My pleasure.' She glanced down at his fingers on her wrist, and then up at his face again. He saw uncertainty but also excitement in her eyes, and knew she was feeling the same inexorable, magnetic pull of desire that he was. 'You're still holding me.'

'That's because I find I don't want to let you go.'

A tiny, uncertain smile curved her mouth. 'You…don't?'

He reached out with his other hand and brushed a stray tendril of hair from her face, tucking it behind her ear, letting his fingers caress her cheek as hers had caressed his. Her skin was soft and cool, like dipping his fingers in water or silk. 'No,' he said softly. 'I don't.'

In one easy movement he anchored his hands on her waist and lifted her up onto his lap. She gasped, her eyes wide with the shock of it. It only took another quick movement to adjust her legs so she was straddling him, her dress rucked up to her thighs, revealing slender, golden legs that were now clasping his.

'There,' Azim said as he settled her more firmly on his lap, his arousal brushing the juncture of her thighs, tantalising him even further. 'That's better.'

'I…' Johara shook her head slowly, her expression dazed but also, Azim thought, inflamed. She gazed down at their bodies pressed together. 'I thought we had to wait until Alazar for…'

'Our wedding night? We do. But that doesn't mean we can't get to know each other a little beforehand.' And he found he wanted to get to know his bride very much. Slowly, being careful not to spook her, he arched his hips so his arousal pressed against her. Johara gasped, clearly shocked by the sensation.

'Does that feel good?' Azim asked, his voice a growl of wanting.

'Yes…' Her breath came out in a shudder and she placed her hands on his shoulders to balance herself, her cheeks flushed, her eyes bright. Azim rocked again and Johara's hands clenched on his shoulders.

'That feels very good,' she admitted in a jagged whisper. 'I don't even know why.' She pressed back against him, her eyes fluttering closed as they rocked against each other for a few incredible seconds, their breathing ragged as they found their rhythm, their bodies pressing into one another in silent, hungry demand.

They'd hardly done anything and yet Azim found he was already close to losing control. Even more intoxicatingly, so was Johara. He wondered how much it would take to push her over the edge, and wanted to do it. He needed to see her fall, to feel her come apart in his arms, under his hands, helpless in her desire for him.

But as much as he longed for that, he knew he had to wait. Wait for the wedding night his country and his position demanded they have. Still, he couldn't keep from sliding one hand along her thigh, the other anchoring her hip, his fingers brushing against her soft centre. Johara's body tensed, her eyes widening.

'*Oh*…but…'

'I do not want to ruin our wedding night,' Azim said in a hoarse voice. 'Merely give you a taste of what we can both look forward to.'

'Oh…' He touched her again, watching as her lips parted, her expression becoming glazed, her hips moving to invite a further caress. She was so open and eager, and it thrilled him. Still he knew he could not risk either of their shame tonight.

Regretfully Azim withdrew his hand, everything in him aching with the desperate need to finish what they'd started, and bury himself deep inside her. He slid his hands up to her face and drew her forward for a thorough, lingering kiss.

Johara melted against him, her body wonderfully pliant and yielding. Azim drew back. 'We will save the rest for our wedding night.' Johara nodded, biting her lip, and Azim saw she could hardly look at him, her face already turning fiery. 'Johara, there is no shame in what we are doing,' he stated, surprised and discomfited by her embarrassment. 'We are married.'

'I know, but...' She shook her head, still not looking at him. 'I didn't know it felt like that.'

'Like what?' Azim asked, bemused. She had a lot more experience ahead of her.

'So...intimate.' She made a face. 'I know I must seem appallingly naïve.'

'Naiveté is no bad thing.' Sometimes he wished he still possessed a little optimistic innocence, the belief that things might actually get better. He'd lost it long, long ago.

'I suppose it's not in a bride who must be a virgin on her wedding night,' she answered with a touch of tartness.

'You still chafe at such restrictions?' The intimacy of the moment was making him feel languidly curious. He wanted to know what she thought as much as he wanted to prolong the moment, the feel of her against him.

'I don't know.' She shifted on his lap, making Azim suppress a groan of sheer longing as her body brushed intimately against him once more. 'Not necessarily, I suppose, but I want more from my life than being an ornament.'

He arched an eyebrow. 'An ornament?'

'The only purpose I have as your wife is to decorate your arm and to secure your throne with my suitability.'

'And to provide an heir.' Azim shifted against her, noting the way her eyes flared with satisfaction. 'That is something we will both enjoy, I think.'

'And yet there can be more to a marriage than this. There should be, anyway.' She gestured to their bodies, a look of confused hurt dawning in her eyes that made him both wary and tense. The warm, drowsy intimacy that had cocooned them started to melt away like a morning mist.

He'd been stupid, he realised. He'd let her in too close, allowed her to see too much. And now, of course, she wanted things. Expected things. Things he had no intention of giving, even if he had the emotional capacity to give them, which he knew he did not.

'It's late.' With only a flicker of regret he straightened her dress and then slid her off his lap. 'You should go.'

'You're dismissing me,' she said, and now he definitely heard the hurt.

'Yes.' With effort he rose from the chair and turned his back on her. 'I am.'

Johara stared at Azim's taut back and knew whatever they had shared was over. Her body was still buzzing from the way he'd touched her, and, far worse, her heart was aching. He'd started to open up to her, told her things, and now he was withdrawing again, becoming as cold and autocratic as ever. He'd touched her as only a husband should and yet now was acting like a stranger. She felt torn between anger and sadness, tears and fury. She'd been stupid to want more from him, to look for it. She'd opened herself up to the kind of rejection she'd told herself she wouldn't let herself feel. *Idiot.*

Slowly she gathered the little bottles of oils and put them back in the case, delaying the moment when she slunk out of here like a scolded servant. After what they'd done, the way he'd touched her body, it felt like an ever worse humiliation, a deeper sorrow.

She couldn't postpone it for ever, though, and Azim clearly had no intention of making it any easier. His back was still to her as he checked his phone; as far as he was concerned, she'd already left. And so, with no other real choice, she did.

Back in her bedroom she got ready for bed, her heart aching even as her body thrummed with remembered pleasure. Every brush of her hands against her over-sensitised skin as she pulled her pyjamas on reminded her of the way Azim had touched her, with such knowing yet gentle expertise. Would their wedding night be like that? Or would Azim act the cold stranger again? Perhaps it would be better for her if he did. Then she wouldn't start hoping again, that crazy optimism inside her insisting they could have more of a relationship than they did—or ever would.

The next morning Azim left for work again before Johara had even arisen. At breakfast she toyed with the eggs on her plate, sipping coffee she didn't really want to drink. It was a gorgeous day, sunny and warm, the sky a brilliant blue. Perfect for sightseeing or simply being in the garden, and Azim had forbidden both. The hours stretched emptily in front of her, made more so by Azim's determined absence.

'Signora Bahjat?'

Johara looked up, startled to see Azim's driver standing in the doorway of the dining room, his cap in his hands. 'Yes?'

'Signor Bahjat asked me to accompany you today. If you would like to see some of Naples's sights.'

'He did?' Johara's jaw nearly dropped in astonishment. Then a smile bloomed across her face as excitement took hold, along with hope. Despite his autocratic dictates of yesterday, he'd chosen to give her this. Perhaps he had softened after last night, even if he had not wanted to act as if he had. And of course that sent her hope soaring again, like a balloon floating into the sky. Still, she wasn't going to question it, at least not now. 'I certainly do,' she said. 'Let me just get my things.'

Azim stood by the front door, watching as the limo pulled up to the entrance. He'd spent a tense day wondering about Johara, hoping she was safe. The decision to allow her to sightsee had been an impulsive one, born of the realisation at how trapped she truly was—and, he acknowledged, the desire to please her. The memory of last night had stayed with him, making him both smile and yearn for more.

Throughout the day he'd wondered what she was doing, if she was enjoying the sights. He'd pictured her strolling through the city, her expression interested and vibrant as she examined a work of art or sipped espresso in a café. A day had never felt so long.

Now he tapped his foot impatiently, watching as Johara exited the car and then ran lightly up the steps, her eyes sparkling like silver stars, her cheeks flushed, a few tendrils of hair falling from her chignon to curl delicately about her face. She looked lovelier than ever, and the sight of her felt like a fist to his solar plexus, making his chest ache not just with desire but something deeper. Something he knew he could not afford to feel.

'Where have you been?' he demanded as she crossed the threshold. The light in her eyes winked out, and Azim cursed himself. He hadn't meant to sound so harsh, but he didn't know how else to be. She disarmed him without even trying, and that was a very unsettling thing. He did not want to give her that kind of power over him, and yet she seemed to take it without even realising.

'Sightseeing, as you instructed me to do.'

'Yes, but you're late.'

'Am I? I had a wonderful time. The frescoes in the cathedral were gorgeous.' She laid one slender hand on his arm, a touch that sent shocks ricocheting right up to his ribcage. 'Thank you, Azim. It was very thoughtful of you to arrange the car and driver.'

Completely disconcerted by her touch and the look in her eyes, he found he could only shrug. 'It was nothing.'

'Even so, it meant something to me.'

Azim stared at her, flummoxed, overwhelmed. It would have been easier to kiss her into silence than respond in kind. As it was he just nodded dismissively and said, 'You should get ready. I am finished my business and we leave for Alazar tonight.'

CHAPTER EIGHT

JOHARA GAZED OUT of the window of the royal jet as the bleak mountains and desert of Alazar's interior came into view. She'd woken up an hour ago in the plane's master bedroom, having spent a restless night wondering what the future held. Azim had remained remote, first immersed in work and then sleeping in the jet's smaller second bedroom. Johara had wondered if he was suffering from another headache, but when she'd asked he'd snapped at her that he was not.

Every terse word or deliberate silence of his felt like a step backwards. She'd been so full of hope, practically buoyant with it, after her day out in Naples. She'd thought Azim was softening, their shared intimacies bringing an even greater and more wonderful intimacy. She'd spun fairy tales in her mind of the two of them learning to get to know one another, being friends, and the hard reality of her cold, remote husband felt like a slap in the face. A stab wound to the heart.

When was she going to learn to stop thinking that way? She needed to set some boundaries, and yet she had no idea how. The things they'd done together, and the things they would do, made boundaries feel impossible. Irrelevant. Every time he touched her she yearned for more. Every time he smiled she started to hope. *Stupid, stupid Johara.*

She glanced at him now, sitting across from her in the main cabin's luxurious seating area, his expression settled in a frown as he scanned some official-looking documents.

'What happens after we leave the plane?' she asked. They were due to arrive in Teruk in less than an hour, and she felt completely unprepared.

Azim glanced up from his papers, his eyebrows still drawn together in a near-scowl. 'We go to the palace.'

'Will there be some…some presentation or ceremony? I mean, since we're formally arriving…'

'Do you want one?'

'No.' She'd rather sneak in without anyone noticing. 'But I want to know what to expect.'

Azim sat back, settling himself more comfortably. 'There will be some press waiting at the airport, no doubt, but I wanted to keep our arrival quiet. The real ceremony will be in two days' time.'

'And what will that look like?'

'One of my staff will brief you.' He returned to scanning his papers, leaving Johara blinking in hurt.

So this was another aspect of a convenient marriage, she supposed. Brisk and businesslike. Except the other night, when she'd been massaging his temples and he'd been touching her, it had been anything but. She told herself it was better this way; it was certainly safer. The trouble was, it didn't *feel* better.

'Why can't you brief me?' she asked, wincing inwardly at the slightly petulant note that had entered her voice.

Azim sighed and looked up from his papers. 'When you arrive at the palace, you will be taken to the harem, where you will remain in seclusion until you appear as a bride.'

She grimaced. 'That sounds about as archaic as everything else.'

'Alazar is a traditional country. You knew this.'

Yes, she had, but she hadn't let herself think about it. She'd pushed the thought of her marriage to Malik far away, pretended it wasn't going to happen. Now the reality was staring her in the face, imminent and unavoidable. 'Why the harem?' she asked. It was a point that had needled her since he'd first mentioned it at their introduction. 'Why can't I live in the normal part of the palace?'

'The harem *is* normal. That,' Azim enunciated, 'is what is normal for Alazar.'

'I thought you were trying to bring the country into the twenty-first century,' Johara shot back. 'Westernise it, at least in some ways. That's what Malik said.'

His eyes flashed and she knew she shouldn't have mentioned Malik. 'Not in that way.' His tone was so flat and final she fell silent, knowing that to ask more questions would be to pick a fight, and the last thing she wanted was more acrimony.

She thought that would be the unfortunate end of it but then Azim sighed and rubbed the bridge of his nose. 'I appreciate that you have essentially grown up in a culture different from the one you were born into. If your father had been sensible, he would have made sure you had spent more time in Alazar, got used to its ways.'

Her father had been so sure of her obedience, he hadn't thought she'd needed to spend time in Alazar. 'I don't understand why things have to be so traditional when you are, by your own admission, trying to modernise the country.'

Azim looked as if he was going to deliver another setdown but then, to her surprise, he answered her question honestly. 'Because the interior of Alazar is controlled by desert tribes who are very traditional, and they are waiting to see how I treat my bride.'

Johara drew back. 'And how do they want you to treat me?'

'They will expect to see you modestly covered and walking several steps behind me when we are in public places, and residing in the women's quarters when you are at home.'

It sounded awful. 'So how exactly are you going to modernise the country, then?' she asked.

'Slowly, at least until the tribes have been appeased. The alternative is civil war, if the tribes start to revolt again.' He paused. 'My brother has been working tirelessly for ten years to keep the country stable. He had achieved that, but my arrival created tension and uncertainty. I must do my best to return the country to its previous stability, and then increase it.' Azim set his jaw, his eyes darkly opaque and hooded, his body radiating tense determination.

'I would have thought your arrival would have brought even more stability,' Johara said after a moment. 'Since you are the firstborn, the true heir.'

'Perhaps in time. But I have been gone a long while. And I spent the last twenty years in a Western country. Some of the tribes doubt my loyalty to Alazaran ways, which makes it even more important that I respect tradition in my personal life.'

Grudgingly Johara had to admit it made sense, even if she didn't quite want it to. 'I suppose I can understand that,' she said after a moment. 'But it would have helped if you'd told me this earlier.'

Azim inclined his head. 'Perhaps I should have.'

She widened her eyes, daring to joke. 'Wait, did you just admit you were wrong?'

'No, only the possibility of it.'

She laughed, even though she wasn't sure if Azim was joking, and then he gave her the glimmer of a smile that lightened her heart. 'So you do have a sense of humour. I was hoping, but I was starting to wonder.'

He rubbed his jaw as his gaze moved to the cerulean sky outside the jet's windows. 'I haven't had much cause for laughing.'

'What did you mean,' Johara asked suddenly, her voice soft and yet intent, 'when you said you were surviving?' She realised she quite desperately wanted to know.

Azim stilled, and then dropped his hand, his gaze returning to his papers. 'Just that.'

'Where did you live?' Johara pressed. 'Who were you with? You were only fourteen, weren't you, when you were kidnapped? Who took care of you?'

'No one.'

'But…what do you mean? Someone must have…'

'Someone who did not do a very good job of it, then,' Azim answered repressively. He let out a long, low breath. 'It was…an unpleasant experience, and one I have no desire to discuss. Now, we are landing shortly, and I need you to change.'

'Change?'

'Wear a hijab and dress suited for your role.' He nodded towards the back of the cabin. 'You will find the appropriate clothes in the bedroom.' His expression was closed and obdurate in a way that was becoming depressingly familiar. Johara knew there was no point in trying to keep conversing now. Azim would give her no answers.

Wordlessly she rose from her seat and went to the bedroom. Laid out on the bed was a hijab of delicate cream lace, and a matching gown that was certainly modest, covering her from her neck to her ankles, but no less pretty for it. Thoughtfully Johara fingered the lace.

Before Azim had confided to her his concerns about Alazar's stability, she would have resisted wearing such a garment. She'd chafed at many of his restrictions, and yet now she could see that some of them at least made sense.

And she was tired of fighting against her fate—she was tired of trying to keep herself independent from the man who, by the dictates of the country he ruled, controlled her. What if she partnered with him instead? What if she gained Azim's trust and confidence by giving him hers? Maybe then they could have some sort of friendship, a way to get along that she could live with and enjoy without getting hurt.

Johara slipped on the dress, the heavy, lace-encrusted material falling about her feet, and adjusted the hijab so it completely covered her hair. She looked in the mirror and was started by her reflection; the lace hijab framed her face, making her eyes appear larger, her lips fuller. She took a deep breath and then went to show herself to Azim.

Approval flared in his eyes as he caught sight of her. 'You look lovely,' he said, and Johara sat back down across from him.

'I am not used to such heavy garments.'

'I know.' He paused. 'Thank you for wearing them.'

A thank you and apology in the course of one morning. Johara almost smiled. Maybe they were actually getting somewhere.

No matter what Johara wore, she looked beautiful and alluring, but Azim thought she looked particularly lovely in the lace hijab and dress, appropriate for a new royal bride. *His* bride. He felt a fierce sense of possession, a need and desire to show her to his country and mark her as his.

Yet thinking of Alazar made familiar tension knot his shoulder blades and pierce his temples. He closed his eyes, willing the pain away. They were going to land in a few minutes, and he could not betray any weakness, knowing his enemies and doubters would seize on it. Now more than ever he needed to be strong.

Then he felt Johara move to sit next to him, her slender, supple body close to his. She pressed something damp, its fragrance sharply familiar, into his hand and he opened his eyes.

'It helps, doesn't it?' she asked softly.

His first impulse was to toss the handkerchief away, to insist he had no need of it and wasn't in pain. It was what he'd done for his entire adult life, because to admit he was suffering was to admit he was weak, and that was one thing he couldn't stand. Not when he'd been forced to be weak, to be utterly pitiful, for so long. Strength, even if it was an illusion, was everything.

Yet sitting there now with Johara so close to him, close enough that he could breathe in her vanilla and almond scent and feel her alluring warmth, her eyes so full of kindness, he found he couldn't do that. He didn't want to, and there was no need, because she had seen him in pain before. She'd seen him in pain and she hadn't thought he was weak. The realisation was like missing a step in a staircase, jolting him, opening him to other, unsettling possibilities.

He pressed the handkerchief to his forehead, breathing in the sharp, clean scent of peppermint. 'Thank you,' he murmured. He was touched by her concern, more than he wanted to admit even to himself. Johara smiled at him, and he managed a smile back. It felt like more than he'd meant to give, as if he'd just declared something to her, and yet he couldn't take it back.

They landed a short while later, and the peppermint oil had, thankfully, staved off the worst symptoms of an oncoming migraine. A few press had gathered by the royal jet as the door opened and the stairs were lowered, poised with cameras and notepads. Johara peeked out of the window, her face pale.

'I've never faced the press before.'

'Haven't you? Your face has been in the Alazaran news enough.'

She stared at him in surprise. 'Has it?'

Azim shook his head slowly. 'You really have lived a sheltered life. Yes, of course it has. You've always been known as the next Sultana, and your wedding to my brother was imminent. Of course you were in the press on occasion.'

'I never knew.'

Which begged the question why her father had kept her so far from Alazar's limelight. Malik had mentioned something about her mother's illness, but Azim had not thought to ask her about it. He had so convinced himself he wasn't interested in getting to know her, didn't need to know. Now he found he wanted to, not just for mere expediency's sake but out of simple—and growing—interest in who she was.

The crowd was waiting, as were the security personnel and motorcade, and Azim knew he would need to leave it for another time.

'You don't need to say anything,' he advised her. 'In fact, you shouldn't. Wave once, keep your head lowered, and follow me to the car.'

The questions rained down on them as soon as they stepped out of the plane. *When was the wedding, what about the rumours they'd already wed and would there still be a ceremony in Alazar?* Azim kept his face politely neutral and said nothing as he stepped past the reporters to the waiting car. He held the door open for Johara and she scooted inside, breathing a sigh of relief when the door shut behind them.

'Will it always be like that?'

'You are a royal, Johara.'

She made a rueful face. 'I don't feel prepared. I know

I have the alleged bloodline—my mother's family is descended from the same princes and kings as yours. But a life in the spotlight is so far from what I've experienced.'

'You won't be in the spotlight very often. Only on certain public occasions.'

'Oh, right, of course.' She glanced out of the window, her wry expression turning into something darker. 'The rest of the time I'll be locked up in the harem.'

Admittedly he'd given her that impression, but now Azim regretted it, at least a little. 'There are no locks on the doors as far as I am aware.'

She managed a brief, tense smile. 'Thank you for putting my mind at ease.'

Irritation warred with sympathy. The sooner his wife accepted the constraints of her new life, the better off they'd both be. 'My pleasure,' he replied, and turned to stare out of the window.

CHAPTER NINE

EVERYTHING WAS A BLUR. It seemed only minutes that they were in the limousine on the way to the palace, and then its golden spires flashed before them. The car had barely stopped before the door was opened and Johara was ushered out to a row of waiting servants who then steered her through the main doors and down several marble corridors before she ended up in a suite of luxurious rooms, behind a set of latticed doors. The harem.

It wasn't as bad as all that, she told herself as she walked around the opulent rooms. Besides a lavish bedroom, she had sitting and dining rooms and a private pool and gym. A table had been set up with fruit, pastries and a pot of mint tea. A young girl, who looked only about fourteen, bobbed a nervous curtsey and asked her if she would like anything else.

'No, this is fine.' Johara gave the girl a reassuring smile. 'What is your name?'

'Aisha, *Sadiyyah.*'

'It is good to meet you.' Johara noticed the girl's chapped-looking fingers as she pleated her hands together. 'Your hands look sore.'

Aisha glanced down at her fingers, blushing. 'It's nothing. They're always like that.'

'Are they?' Johara reached out to examine the girl's hand, glancing up at her. 'May I?'

'Of—Of course, *Sadiyyah*.'

It looked like eczema, and could be treated with a salve of coconut oil and jojoba. Johara was about to offer to make some up when she realised that of course she couldn't. She didn't have her garden here, her stillroom with its stove and all her equipment for making oils and other natural concoctions. She gave Aisha a sympathetic smile. 'I'll see if I can get some proper salve for you.'

The girl beamed. 'Thank you, *Sadiyyah*.'

It wasn't going to be so bad here, Johara told herself as she readied for bed that night, trying to be as optimistic as she could. She'd eaten dinner by herself, served by Aisha, who had, after some shy hesitation, shared a little bit about herself. They'd had a pleasant chat about palace life, and Aisha had assured her she could order anything she wanted and she would have it almost instantly.

An ice cream sundae, a favourite book or DVD, a new dress. Anything, and yet nothing at all. The restrictions reminded her of her father's empty gifts, lovely, dazzling even, and yet ultimately costing nothing. The things she truly wanted—the freedom to choose her own destiny, the affection or at least the company of the man she'd married—were utterly beyond her request or reach.

She did not see Azim for two endless days. Days that were kept busy with preparations for her wedding and yet which felt far too long. She wanted to see Azim, needed to reassure herself that the man she'd had glimpses of before, a man who was taciturn but also kind, was still there, or had really existed at all.

When she'd asked Aisha about where Azim was, the girl had looked scandalised. 'He cannot see you before the wedding day!' she'd exclaimed, and then scurried off.

Johara had fought exasperation and even tears, and then chosen laughter instead. He couldn't see her, when he'd already kissed her senseless and far more? Just the memory of his hands on her made her blush. She'd never felt anything so intimate, so intense, before; she both thrilled and trembled to think of feeling it again—and more.

Even from behind the palace doors Johara could feel the buzz of the palace as the wedding drew closer. Servants came and went, chattering excitedly, bringing cloth and jewels and perfumes, trying out different necklaces and earrings, and in spite of her trepidation she found herself caught up in the mood.

She stood still for fittings of her ornate wedding dress, encrusted with pearls and trimmed with a yard of lace, that was appropriately modest and yet also the most gorgeous thing she'd ever seen.

'His Highness chose this cloth for you specially,' the seamstress told her, and Johara stared at her in surprise.

'He did?'

'Yes, on the day your engagement was announced, when you first came to Alazar.'

When she'd run away. Guilt curdled her insides. Azim had made a kind gesture and she'd essentially trampled on it. Now, gazing at her reflection in the mirror, she wondered what Azim would think when he saw her in it, if his eyes would flare with male appreciation and desire. She pictured him slipping the cream hijab from her head, unpinning her hair, taking off her dress…

'Don't fidget,' the seamstress reprimanded her, and Johara saw her reflection give a secret smile. As the days stretched on, she found she couldn't wait for her wedding, simply for this limbo to be over—and so she could see Azim again.

* * *

Today was his wedding day. Azim studied his reflection in the mirror, straightening the jewelled collar of the brocade *jubba* he wore, paired with matching trousers. It was the traditional wedding outfit for a sultan, and it felt heavy and stiff across his shoulders, reminding him of Johara's comment about her unfamiliar clothing.

There was much she wasn't used to here, and he wondered how she was receiving it all. How had she found the harem, after all her protestations? Was she looking forward to their wedding, now that she'd had a taste of the pleasures they both would know?

It had felt like an endless two days without her, busy as he'd been learning the politics of his kingdom with Malik at his right hand. His grandfather had become too ill to do much more than bark from his bed, for which Azim was grateful. He tried to avoid the old man as much as possible. The memories he had of him were nearly all bitter.

Although he knew the separation was an important part of the Alazaran wedding tradition, he wished he'd had a chance to see Johara before the ceremony. Why, he couldn't even say. It seemed as if every attempt to reassure her failed, and in any case it was far better to start the way they were meant to go on, living virtually separate lives. And yet since that encounter in his bedroom, when she'd touched him so gently, when he'd felt her unrestrained response, he wasn't at all sure that was what he wanted any more.

The trouble was, he didn't know what he wanted—or how to get it.

'Your Highness?' An attendant appeared at the doorway of his bedroom. 'It is time.'

Azim nodded and turned away from his reflection. Indeed, it was time.

The grand salon of the palace was full of dignitaries and diplomats as Azim took his place at the front, his expression grave as he looked towards the back of the room from where Johara would proceed. He wondered what she looked like, if she was excited or nervous or still, heaven help them both, reluctant. Today she would stand in front of all of Alazar and take him as her husband of her own free will, the *nikkah* ceremony that was an essential part of any marriage. Today he would truly claim his bride.

Johara took a deep breath and tried to stem the tide of nervousness that threatened to overwhelm her. There were so many people. After spending two days in virtual isolation in the harem, she wasn't prepared for the sheer noise and size of the wedding ceremony. Or the sight of Azim at the other end of the room, looking more remote than ever in a brocade *jubba* and trousers, his expression seeming as if it had been hewn from stone.

Everything in her resisted this step, even though she knew she had no choice. They were already married, after all. Still she hesitated, caught on the cusp of knowing she was starting down an irrevocable path that would lead on to for ever.

Then Azim caught sight of her, and for the merest second his mouth flicked upwards. A smile. Her husband, her groom, was smiling at her, offering her the reassurance she'd been craving. Relief poured through her, and, even though his expression had turned severe again, Johara kept that smile like a secret, tucked away in her heart. She started down the aisle.

Each step felt weighted down by the heavy dress as well as the stares of several hundred people. Trying not to notice, she kept her head held high, her gaze fixed on Azim. She willed him to smile again, but his expression did not change and she almost faltered. Then, at the last step, Azim reached out with his hand and drew her towards him. The feel of his palm sliding across and then encasing hers gave Johara the strength to stand tall as the ceremony began, the words washing over her, barely audible over the hard thud of her heart. Then a question, said a bit louder, reverberated through her.

'Do you consent to this marriage of your own free will?'

This was the *nikkah,* the required part of the ceremony where they both pledged their freely given commitment to the marriage. She glanced at Azim, who was staring straight ahead, his jaw tense, his gaze shuttered. Johara realised she knew that look. He was bracing himself, thinking she might refuse. And yet how could she?

For a second, no more, she considered what would happen if she *did* refuse. Scandal, humiliation for Azim, instability for Alazar. Could she request an annulment of their marriage? Would she be thrown out from her father's house, having to make her way on the street?

But she *could* do it, she realised, just as Azim had pointed out. She could refuse. In this moment the choice was hers. Her destiny was her own, even if it hadn't felt like it. She was free to do as she pleased. And she knew what she wanted. That smile had given her hope, had made her believe. *This could work.*

Azim squeezed her hand, the pressure gentle but firm, and she realised she was taking too long to answer the question. A question she knew the answer to, even as so much of her future remained uncertain. 'Yes,' she said. 'I do so consent.'

CHAPTER TEN

IT WAS HER wedding night. Servants chattered and giggled around her as they prepared Johara for Azim, giving her knowing smiles and winks, making her blush. She'd already been bathed like a baby, fragrant oils massaged into her skin, intricate patterns of henna painted on her hands and feet. Her hair had been arranged in heavy coils and loops, her face carefully painted. And then they'd presented her with a nightgown that looked nearly transparent, the scalloped lace barely covering her breasts. Johara had stared at it, fascinated and appalled.

'But…but there's hardly anything to it!'

Basima, Aisha's mother, had giggled. 'Exactly why your husband will like it so much,' she'd said, and slipped it over Johara's head.

Fortunately a much more modest robe of gold satin accompanied it, but Johara still felt terribly bare. She'd thought she would be better prepared for this, considering what she and Azim had already done together, and yet now that the moment had arrived she realised afresh how little she'd actually shared with him. One kiss, one caress. Intense experiences both, but hardly enough preparation for *this*. She'd barely spoken to him throughout the wedding ceremony and celebration; they'd sat on matching thrones, drinking *sharbat* as a dozen different people, all of them important and officious, had toasted their marriage, their health, even their fertility. But Azim had hardly said anything at all. He'd barely even looked at her, and Johara had kept sneaking him glances, craving reassurance, something more than the tiny smile he'd given her as she'd walked down the aisle. Something that assured her she'd made the right choice in consenting, in believing that they could actually have some sort of real marriage. A real friendship.

'And now it is time.' Basima clapped her hands and stepped aside, and Johara's mother approached her, her smile fixed, her eyes as blank as ever. Naima had long ago stopped registering any emotion or interest in the world, and she approached this momentous event as she would any other, small or large, with a staring face and a distant air, as if she weren't actually there.

Johara had not seen her since she'd arrived in Alazar, beyond a few distant glimpses at the wedding ceremony and celebration. She'd long ago stopped hoping for anything from Naima, a loving word or glance, had thought she'd come to terms with her emotional absence, but she felt it keenly now.

'May God bless your union,' Naima said, and kissed her, cool lips brushing her forehead. Johara gazed into her mother's face, wishing Naima would smile and reassure her. Wondering if her mother had felt this uncertain on her own wedding night. *Love is a facile emotion.* Had her mother known her father's thoughts on the matter when she'd married? If only Johara could ask her, seek some wisdom on how to navigate marriage without love.

'Thank you, Maman,' she whispered, and Naima stepped away, her duty dispatched. She was leaving for France in the morning, and Johara didn't know when she would see her again. Everything that felt familiar was gone. All that was left was Azim.

Taking a deep breath, accompanied by a host of female attendants, Johara started towards her husband's bedroom.

Azim heard the excited clamour of female voices coming from the hallway and he tensed. He'd been anticipating this moment ever since he'd first kissed Johara, had spent several sleepless nights imagining it in all of its enticing splendour, but now that he was here he felt as unsure as a boy.

The ceremony earlier had been rich in pomp and ritual, and Azim had played his part—but that was what it had felt like, a part. He'd been strangely detached from everything, watching Johara, seeing how young and nervous she had looked, noting his grandfather's narrowed gaze, the way Malik had held Gracie's hand. This was his life now, his home, his people, and yet he felt as if he were spinning in a void, alone. Always alone. He didn't know how to be anything else, and he wondered if he ever would. If he would ever dare to try for something different, something dangerous.

Tonight was about being as close to a person as you could possibly be, and yet he felt more isolated than ever, conscious of all the gaping years of loneliness and revenge that had consumed him, the scars on his back he still wouldn't allow Johara to see, the wounds in his heart. He'd barricaded himself from the rest of humanity because letting people in was giving them access to your weakness, showing them how to slip the knife between the ribs, into the heart.

Yet so far Johara had seen glimpses and she hadn't shied away. She hadn't thought he was weak. No, she'd wanted *more*. She'd asked more questions, craved more closeness. The knowledge surprised him, alarmed him too.

And pleased him, because part of him knew he wanted to be known. However stupid that was.

The women knocked at the door and tersely Azim bid them to enter. They spilled in, laughing and giggling, eyes downcast, pushing Johara forward. She stumbled slightly on the hem of her robe and then righted herself, looking up, blushing, at Azim, her gaze darting away before he'd had time to offer a smile, although in truth he didn't know if he could.

The women were backing away, flapping their hands, offering encouragement, their only chance to be ribald. Finally one of the older women shooed them out, and the door closed with a decisive click. They were alone.

Johara was still staring at her feet, her slender body encased in a satin robe, her hair done up in intricate loops of shining blue-black.

Azim cleared his throat. 'You look lovely.'

'Thank you.' Her voice was a husky whisper. Azim could see her body tremble. If he felt unsure and a little nervous, he could not begin to imagine how his bride might be feeling, having been pushed into the room like a human sacrifice, as innocent in this as in everything else.

'A drink,' he said decisively. He'd ordered a bottle of champagne, and now he popped the cork and poured them two glasses. They both needed to relax.

Johara looked up, her eyes widening, wide and silvery and as clear as glacier lakes. 'I've never tasted champagne.'

'Surely now is the perfect opportunity.'

She nodded, accepting a glass, and then taking a sip and wrinkling her nose. 'Fizzy.'

He smiled, amused and also touched by her honest, unhidden responses to everything. 'Indeed.'

She looked up, her expression heartbreakingly candid. 'This all feels so strange.'

'Yes.'

'Look.' She showed him one palm, hennaed with intricate designs. 'It took hours.'

'It is beautiful.'

'I feel as if I've been trussed up like a chicken.' She laughed, and the sound, so tinkling and genuine, made him smile again. 'It's all a bit ridiculous, isn't it? All the ritual?'

'Traditions exist for a reason.'

'Yes.' She took another sip of champagne. 'I suppose they do. I suppose it makes people happy, to see it all done properly, the way it's been done for centuries. Will the Bedouin tribes be satisfied by all this, do you think?'

'I hope so.' When Azim had returned to the palace Malik had given him a report; the tribes were muttering, wondering if he was too European, displeased by his unexpected trip to France and Italy. They doubted whether he would continue to do things the old way. The negotiations with their leaders would require patience and discretion, otherwise Alazar could be plunged into civil unrest yet again. But he didn't want to think about Alazar now.

Johara wandered around the room, her robe swishing around her legs. He could see the outline of her breasts underneath the satin, and his body stirred insistently. 'Is this your bedroom?' she asked.

'Yes.'

She glanced at the canopied king-sized bed on its dais, piled high with satin coverlets embroidered in rich colours. Her gaze swept over it and then the whole room thoughtfully. 'Nothing about this room reveals you.'

He started, disconcerted by her remark. The last thing he wanted to be was *revealed*. 'Why should it?'

She turned to him with a little shrug. 'Because it's your bedroom. Your private room.'

'I've only been in the palace for a matter of weeks.'

'Yes, but a book or a picture, at least? Something. Most people would have something.'

He shrugged, feeling uncomfortably exposed by her perception. He was not most people.

'And there wasn't anything personal that I could see in Naples, either.'

'It is true, I do not have a lot of personal effects.'

For those first few years in Naples he'd had nothing but the ragged clothes on his back. Afterwards, he had never seen the point of keepsakes, mementoes, meaningful trinkets. Houses, cars, yachts—these things he possessed, because they had value in of themselves. They could be bought or sold, assessed and admired. And none of them were special. If you didn't let things become important, it wouldn't matter if they were taken away. And he'd had everything taken away, once.

'I can't decide,' Johara said slowly, 'if you are hiding yourself, or if it is simply that there is nothing to hide.' She stared at him openly, waiting for him to respond. Azim had no idea what to say.

Nothing to hide? He had far too much to hide. Scars, wounds, darkness, shame. Nothing he wanted Johara to see, and yet as she looked at him with that soft, silvery gaze he felt as if she saw it already, she was already starting to know him, and in that moment he didn't know how that made him feel.

'I don't have photographs,' he said, 'because there has been no one in my life worth remembering.'

Her eyes widened, her mouth turning down in surprised sympathy. 'No one?' He shrugged. 'What about your parents?'

'My father was a weak man who fell apart after my mother died.'

'She died when you were young,' Johara recalled slowly.

'When I was six. But I rarely saw her, or my father.'

'You were raised by your grandfather.'

'Yes.'

'He seems a hard man.'

Azim felt his jaw tense. 'Yes.'

'And your brother?' she asked softly. 'Were you ever close to him?'

For a moment he pictured Malik as a boy, all floppy dark hair and soulful eyes. He could see them both, lying on their stomachs, building a model aeroplane together. He could hear the laughter carried on the breeze, and he could almost, *almost* feel the lightness inside him that he'd felt then. But then it was as if a dark cloud hovering on the horizon moved closer, blotting everything out.

'Once.'

'Do you think you could be again?'

'Perhaps.' He didn't want to admit that he didn't know if he had it in him. If the softness and sympathy had been leached out of him by so many years alone.

Johara put her hands on slender hips. 'So no photos. What about books?'

'I don't read,' he said, and her eyebrows rose.

'Don't…?'

'I can read,' he clarified impatiently, 'but I try not to. Reading for business is about all I can manage. For pleasure…' He shook his head.

Realisation dawned in her eyes. 'Your headaches.'

'Yes.' He had no idea why he'd told her all that. Perhaps because he'd wanted her to understand something of him, to know that he wasn't a cipher, someone who wasn't interesting or alive or fully human. For too long he'd lived like a ghost or a shadow, but tonight he wanted to be real. He wanted to feel.

'Have you seen a doctor about it?' she asked.

'They say there is nothing they can do. In any case I have learned to live with the pain. Sometimes it feels like a part of me. Something that were it to stop, I would no longer be myself.' He could hardly believe he was saying the words, revealing so much, and yet bizarrely he wanted her to understand. To know. *Him.*

'Experience defines and shapes us,' she agreed quietly. 'But its end surely does not mean our own.'

'Perhaps.' He wasn't sure about that; if he took away the pain, the suffering, the hardship, what would be left? Not much, he feared. His success, his wealth, his whole self had been built on those foundations. They had defined him for too long.

She cocked her head. 'You are not convinced.'

'Perhaps you need to convince me.' He had an overwhelming desire to touch her, to feel that connection they'd once experienced before. 'Come here,' he said, and then he reached for her.

Her hand felt soft and small in his as he drew her slowly to him. She stood in front of him, the rise and fall of her breasts as she breathed visible beneath the thin satin of her robe and gown. She looked up at him, her eyes wide and clear, full of trust—trust he didn't know if he deserved, but in that moment he wanted to earn it.

He lifted her hand, his thumb sliding along her palm, and kissed the delicate skin of her inner wrist. He felt a tremor go through her—and himself. 'I've been wanting to touch you again. Very much.'

Johara's wrist flexed under his lips, and when she spoke her voice was a breathy whisper. 'I've been wanting to be touched.'

'You're not afraid?'

'No. Not afraid.' A shudder went through her. 'Nervous, perhaps.'

'You do not need to be nervous.' He touched her fingers to her chin, tilting her face upwards so he could meet her gaze. 'I will not hurt you.'

'But it does hurt, doesn't it?' She spoke practically, looking to him for both honesty and reassurance.

'A little, or so I've been told.' He gave her the glimmer of a smile. 'I do not know myself.'

'When did you lose your virginity?'

He laughed, disconcerted and yet also a little charmed by the blunt question. 'A long time ago.'

'I shouldn't have asked.' She bit her lip. 'Sorry.'

'No, no.' He shrugged. 'Sadly, it wasn't memorable. A single encounter.'

'Do you remember her?'

He pictured a knowing smile, a sultry look, nothing more. 'Barely.'

She nodded slowly, accepting, and he felt strangely shamed by the admission, as if it were something to be sad about, to regret. Perhaps it was. Heaven knew he hadn't experienced much of women beyond what they could provide him for a few brief hours. This experience was, in some ways, as new to him as it was to Johara, and the depth of it entirely unexpected.

'More champagne,' he said, and filled both their glasses.

She let out a shaky laugh as she took a sip. 'You're going to get me drunk.'

'Two glasses of champagne shouldn't accomplish that.' He definitely did not want her drunk. A little buzzy and relaxed, yes.

She twirled the flute between her fingers. 'I've never had much alcohol before. A glass of wine, perhaps, when my father visited.'

Which made him remember what he'd wanted to ask. 'Your mother is ill,' he said, phrasing it somewhere between a statement and a question as he drew her to a set of comfortable chairs by the window.

'Ill? Yes.' Her gaze was shadowed, a little wary, as she looked out at the palace now lost in twilit shadows. 'You could say that.'

'What is the illness?'

Her throat worked for a moment and she rotated the fragile stem of her champagne flute with slender fingers. 'Depression.'

'Ah.' He paused, the realisation sinking into him. He'd seen Naima Behwar only briefly at the ceremony, and it occurred to him now how little she'd engaged with her daughter, her only child, or in fact with anyone. He hadn't remarked it at the time because who was he to notice such things? He'd had an utter lack of loving relationships in his life. But now, looking at Johara's sad face, her thoughtful frown, he thought he understood, at least a little. 'That is why your father sent you both to France?'

'She prefers it there,' Johara answered quickly, instantly defensive, and then she sighed, her shoulders slumping a little. 'Yes, I suppose. He never said exactly, but...' She shrugged, staring down into the popping bubbles of her champagne. 'I suppose it became apparent. Obvious. She was an embarrassment to him, a liability to his ambition. We were never to talk about it.'

'And that is why you have not returned to Alazar very often.'

'Only for the most formal, necessary occasions.' Her smile was both sad and wry, and it reached him like a fist around his heart. 'I didn't realise it for a long time. Why he kept us in France. I didn't see it that way, that it was...a banishment. I simply accepted it as the way things were. I was so *trusting*.' A savage note of despair had entered her voice, torn on the last word, and she shook her head, her eyes full of recrimination and memory.

'Your father was not worthy of your trust?' Azim surmised, and Johara shook her head again, harder this time.

'No.'

From what he'd experienced of Arif Behwar he wasn't exactly surprised, but he was curious all the same as to how Johara had arrived at that conclusion. 'Why do you say this now?'

'Because…' She froze, her expression turning trapped, her eyes wide with sudden realisation.

'Johara…?' His voice was gentle but a cold finger of realisation had begun a relentless creep along his spine.

'Because,' she whispered, 'he insisted I marry you.' The smile she gave him was lopsided, uncertain, as if hoping he'd see the funny side of it. Or not.

Azim felt his expression iron out, like a mask slipping over his face, over his true self. 'You asked him to reconsider our marriage.' It was a statement, coolly given. Why it should hurt or even surprise him, he did not know. He knew how reluctant she'd been. She'd run away, for heaven's sake. And yet stupidly perhaps, it still stung.

'Yes, but only because…because I didn't know you.'

And she didn't know him now, not really. Azim leaned back in his chair. 'I see.'

'You don't, not really,' Johara insisted. 'Because…because I feel differently now.'

Of course she would say that. And of course she would confuse lust with something deeper, something like love. Hell, this evening he'd practically been doing it as well. And yet at the same time the soft and stupidly tender feelings he'd been nurturing for these last few moments were rapidly evaporating, replaced by a determination to keep this what it was supposed to be—and nothing more.

'Well.' He plucked the glass out of her hand and put it with his own on a nearby table. 'It is done, at any rate.'

Johara gazed at him, anxious now. 'Are you angry?'

'No, why should I be? Your reluctance to this marriage was clear, Johara.' He smiled at her, determined to stay both relaxed and unmoved. What she'd felt about their marriage didn't matter. He wouldn't let it matter. 'But I think,' he continued in an inexorable tone, 'the time has come for us to put words aside.'

CHAPTER ELEVEN

AZIM'S EXPRESSION WAS OBDURATE, his smile like steel. The warm feeling that had enveloped Johara, of relaxation and comfort, of understanding and being understood, had evaporated, replaced by something that both alarmed and thrilled her.

'Already…?'

'It is our wedding night, Johara.' Azim's eyes blazed darkly. 'This has to happen.'

'I know.' Still she didn't move. She couldn't. She was paralyzed by anxiety, even as a strange, surprising excitement licked along her veins. She remembered his kiss, the way his mouth had plundered hers so thoroughly, the sparks of pleasure he'd ignited inside her, the roaring flame that had only just begun to burn.

And then when he'd touched her…his fingers so knowing, so *intimate*. Yet what had been amazing and intense now made her blush in remembrance.

'Johara.' Azim's voice was rough and gentle at the same time. He looked devastatingly attractive, stubble glinting on his jaw, the loose linen shirt he wore open at the throat, revealing a column of brown throat and a tantalising glimpse of his muscular chest, sprinkled with springy dark hair. 'I promised you, I will not hurt you.' He held out his hand and Johara stared at the callused palm, the long, lean fingers, knowing she would have to take this step and yet still resisting.

They'd only just begun to talk. She'd only just begun to know him—and to start to like what she knew. And then she'd ruined it by admitting she hadn't wanted to marry him. Something he knew, of course, and yet it had spoiled the mood, or at least created another one. One of sensual, sexual expectation. She saw the heat in Azim's eyes and felt burned by it.

She wasn't ready for this. To give herself to him, to bare herself so utterly, felt like a leap into the unknown, and she had no idea how high the drop or hard the fall. And yet he was her *husband*. She knew her duty. This was his right, just as it was hers. Just as he'd said, this had to happen.

Slowly she reached out and took his hand. She felt as if she were sleepwalking as he drew her from her chair and led her slowly to the bed, his dark, hot gaze not leaving hers. Her pulse hammered wildly in her throat and her breath came in shallow pants even though he had barely touched her. They'd barely begun.

Her feet sank into thick, plush carpet as she stared at him, waiting for him to touch her. To tell her what to do, because she had no idea.

Gently Azim touched the pulse at her throat with one finger. 'You are scared.'

'A little,' she admitted in a whisper.

'May I?' He reached for the sash of her robe. Holding her breath, Johara nodded. He tugged at the sash and the robe opened, revealing her negligee, which was near-transparent, the sexiest and most revealing thing she'd ever worn, the deep V neckline plunging low enough to reveal most of her breasts, her nipple visible through the scalloped lace. The silk was gossamer-thin and showed every shadow and curve. She might as well be naked. Soon she would be.

Azim had dimmed the lights and drawn the curtains across the oncoming twilight, so the room was bathed in warm light and comforting shadows. Even so she felt exposed, her body open to his intense gaze. Johara swallowed audibly.

Slowly his eyes swept over her, and his mouth tightened and a muscle flickered in his cheek as he finished his thorough inspection, missing nothing. It felt as he were physically touching her with his gaze, burning the secret places barely concealed. His gaze finally moved to her face and settled there. 'Will you undo your hair?'

Self-consciously she reached up to the heavy mass of hair pinned at the back of her neck with its intricate loops and whorls. She started to withdraw a pin and then stopped. 'It is a husband's privilege to undo his wife's hair.'

'So it is.' He didn't move and Johara looked at him uncertainly, finding it hard to dare even in this.

'Do you want to…?'

'Yes,' he said, the word simple and sincere, and he moved towards her. Johara remained still, her breathing going shallow again as he stood before her and lifted his hands to her hair. His breath fanned her face and she closed her eyes, bowing her head a little so he could take out the pins more easily.

Each brush of his fingers against her skin sent tiny electric shocks skittering along her nerve endings. Each slide of a pin from her hair felt incredibly intimate, strangely erotic, causing a tendril of hair to uncoil and fall down her back.

He plucked one pin out after another, tossing them onto the top of the bureau where they scattered, the only sound in the room besides their increasingly ragged breathing.

Another pin and then her hair was free, and all of it fell down her back in a dark river of tumbled waves and curls, well past her waist.

Azim picked it up in two handfuls, bringing it to his face to breathe in the vanilla scent of her shampoo. 'It's so long.'

'It's never been cut.'

He looked up in surprise. 'Never?'

She shook her head. 'My mother thought it should grow longer. When she married her hair fell to her knees. But mine stopped growing.'

'It is more than long enough for me.' He drew it back over her shoulders, smoothing one hand down its shining length. 'It's beautiful.' The words sounded stilted, as if he wasn't used to paying compliments. Johara certainly wasn't used to receiving them.

She liked her face well enough, but she didn't think she was traditionally beautiful, at least not by Alazar's standards of feminine beauty. She was too tall, her nose too long, her mouth too wide, her jaw too firm.

'Thank you,' she whispered. She thought he must be able to see her heart pounding through the thin nightgown. She could certainly feel it.

Azim wrapped one thick tendril of hair around his wrist and pulled her closer to him. Their hips bumped and she drew her breath in sharply at the feel of his arousal pressing insistently against the softness of her belly.

He released her hair, moving it so her neck was bare. Then he bent his head and pressed a kiss to the sensitive curve of her neck, making her gasp again. He nipped her skin softly with his teeth, the tiny sting of pain somehow making the pleasure all the sweeter. Her knees buckled and she grabbed onto his shoulder for balance.

He laughed softly, the sound full of satisfaction. 'I like how you respond to me.'

'I don't know what I'm doing,' she confessed in a rush. 'What I'm feeling.' It was the same torrent of sensations she'd felt before, only stronger. She felt as if she were melting from the middle, a deep, instinctive longing rising up inside her, controlling her actions, begging for more.

Azim kissed her again, light, butterfly kisses up to her ear, and then he sucked gently on her earlobe, which seemed the strangest and yet most wonderful thing. Her fingernails dug into his shoulder as she tilted her head to give him better access.

'You don't need to know,' Azim told her. He was working his way round to her mouth, and Johara was possessed with the sudden, intense need, a craving she'd felt like no other, to have his lips on hers. 'Just let yourself feel it.' He paused, his lips almost brushing hers. 'Feel it all,' he said, and then his mouth was on hers, claiming it, claiming her, her very soul seeming sucked into that kiss.

She grabbed onto his shirt to anchor herself, drowning in his kiss, revelling in the feel of him even as her senses exploded. It was too much. She felt as if he were possessing her, as if she'd lost who she was apart from that kiss.

Azim broke the kiss, his gaze hot and hard on hers, to slide the straps of her nightgown off her shoulders and down her arms, and Johara shivered in the cool night air as the garment pooled at her feet.

She was naked, every part of her bare to him. A rosy blush spread across her entire body and Johara looked down, embarrassed by her own nudity, feeling more vulnerable than she ever had in her life.

Azim cupped her breast in one large palm, running his thumb gently over the peak. The touch felt shocking, as if he were taking hold not just of one part but her whole self. Owning her. 'You are beautiful.'

Johara released the breath she'd been holding in a relieved shudder. His hand was warm and sure on her breast, his thumb moving in lazy circles that created tremors through her whole body. She wanted to back away; she wanted him to touch her more. 'I'm glad you think so,' she whispered.

Azim cupped both of her breasts in his palms and Johara closed her eyes, amazed at how his touch could turn her to liquid, everything in her melting and straining at the same time. He slid his hands to her waist, spanning it easily, and pulled her more closely to him, so his erection throbbed and pulsed against her, an insistent life force.

Another shudder went through her, and her hips moved of their own accord, pressing back against him, welcoming him into the juncture of her thighs. Wanting him there. She was learning the steps of a dance she'd never known, and yet her body seemed to know them clumsily, instinctively.

Azim let out a groan as he fastened his hands on her hips, anchoring her in place, his arousal throbbing against her.

'Slowly,' he murmured, and then, placing one strong arm under her knees, he scooped her up as if she were no more than a handful of air and laid her on the bed.

Johara pressed back against the silken sheets, conscious of how naked she was, how on display. Then her eyes widened as Azim began to undress, lean fingers flicking open the buttons of his shirt, revealing more and more bronzed chest. The buttons finished, he shrugged off the garment, showing a torso that rivalled any Grecian statue in its perfect musculature, his burnished skin sprinkled with dark hair that veed downwards. The trousers came off next, in a gentle snick of sound, and he kicked them away. His hips were slim, his legs muscular and sprinkled with dark hair, and when he slid his boxers off she averted her eyes, overwhelmed by the sight of him wholly naked.

'You have nothing to fear,' he murmured, and joined her on the bed.

The collision of their naked bodies as he drew her into his arms was both sweet and strange, soft meeting hard, smooth touching rough. She felt each aching point of contact, her nipples brushing the hard wall of his chest, her hip bone pressing into his thigh, their legs loosely twined.

He slid his hand from her shoulder to her hip, smoothing his way across her skin, and then his fingers drifted to her leg, stroking the tender flesh of her inner thigh, creating quivers of sensation. Johara tensed, remembering how glorious this had felt before. It felt even better now, combined with the heady sensations of his naked body against hers. His fingers brushed her centre and she felt as if she'd been electrocuted. She jumped and Azim laughed softly.

'Why does it feel so good?' she murmured, dazed by the way his fingers moved with such knowing deftness, creating ripples of pleasure so intense Johara let out a mewling sound she'd never heard herself make before.

'I don't think many people care about that answer,' Azim murmured. He spread her thighs farther apart, his touch becoming deeper and more knowing, each stroke bringing Johara another stronger wave of pleasure.

Then he lowered his head and to her utter shock she felt his lips on her, his tongue touching her with the same deft surety. Her hips arched instinctively and she closed her eyes, embarrassed at how exposed she was, how revealing the act even as pleasure overwhelmed her. How did people do this and then look each other in the face?

How could she face Azim when he knew how he affected her, how he played her body like an instrument and only he knew the tune?

Her legs were splayed wide open, Azim's mouth exploring her most intimate folds. Johara let out a sound that was half moan, half sob. The sensations were building inside her, like a towering wave that was about to come crashing down, more intense than anything she'd ever felt before. She didn't know whether to welcome the deluge or run away from it.

'Let yourself feel it, Johara,' Azim instructed, his voice harsh with his own wanting. 'Let yourself go.'

'How...?' The word was a cry, everything inside her coiled so tightly she felt as if she might come apart, and she was afraid what would happen if she did. She could see a shining light but it felt too hot, too bright, and Azim was commanding that she walk towards it. That she let it burn her up.

'Trust me,' Azim murmured, his mouth and fingers continuing to work their magic, touching her more deeply, and her body pulsed around him as her hips arched and the sensations exploded inside her.

Her mind blanked with bright light as her body took over, the pleasure exquisite and almost painful in its intensity, wave after wave crashing over her until they were mere ripples, her body juddering with each one. She let out a gasp as she clutched at Azim, pressing her damp forehead against his shoulder. She felt weak, her muscles loose and relaxed, her body limp and pulsing with the aftershocks of a climax far stronger than anything she'd ever experienced before.

She felt overcome and emotional, weirdly near tears, moved by the entire experience. She craved Azim's closeness, not just his body, but his mind and even his heart.

How could anyone do this and not crave that kind of closeness? One without the other felt absurd, wrong.

'There is much more to it than that,' Azim told her, a hint of humour in his voice, a note of raw, sexual satisfaction. He rolled her onto her back, bracing himself above her. Johara blinked up at him, saw the look of harsh and sensual intent in his face, and felt herself quail.

There was no softening in Azim's features, no breaching of his mind or heart in this moment. This was a physical exercise of intense pleasure, nothing more. Her body might be ready, slick and wanting, but her mind felt suspended emotionally, needing more from Azim than his assured ability to awaken her to desire.

She tensed, her hands clutching his shoulders, as his arousal nudged her entrance. She clamped her lips together as he began to enter her, the invasion so unexpected, so *much*, it brought tears stinging to her eyes. Films and novels didn't do this justice. No one said how intimate it all was, how exposing and overwhelming. He was invading her soul. She bit her lip, her eyes scrunched closed.

'Am I hurting you?' Azim asked, his voice a growl of barely held self-control.

'No.' He wasn't, not in that way. The feel of him inside her was strange, parts of her stretching in a way that felt utterly alien, but it didn't *hurt*. And yet something did, because she felt nearer to tears than ever before, her mind resisting this closeness, her body demanding it, her hips arching up to receive and welcome him.

Azim slid all the way inside her, taking her over. In that moment he owned her, and he knew it. She saw it in the way he smiled, the satisfaction and triumph that blazed in his eyes as he began to move. She moved her hips in rhythm with his, needing to, finding it clumsily, and then becoming more assured. Each stroke brought a fresh wave of pleasure until that was all there was, all she could feel, her body's need obliterating her mind's protest. Her cry, when she came, was a jagged plea that broke on the still air, left her in splinters.

Azim sagged on top of her for one moment and Johara stroked his damp, spiky hair, still trying for the kind of intimacy that she knew Azim didn't want to give. He'd made her body sing but her heart yearned—and his was cold.

Her hands began to drift down his back and in one fluid movement Azim rolled off the bed and away from her, shrugging on a dressing gown before Johara could blink, and then disappearing into the bathroom, leaving her feeling achingly alone even as her body still hummed with her sated desire.

CHAPTER TWELVE

AZIM GAZED IN the bathroom mirror at his own flushed face,
eyes glittering, and wondered why he didn't feel more satisfied. He'd made Johara respond, just as he'd known she
would. Watching her come apart under his touch had been
a sweet satisfaction. And afterwards…he'd found his own
pleasure, deeply, and he knew she had as well. He'd got
exactly what he'd wanted from the experience.

And yet, as his heart rate slowed and his breathing
evened, it wasn't the memory of the savage, intense pleasure he'd just enjoyed that pulsed through his brain. It was
the memory of Johara looking up at him with such innocence and trust as he'd taken down her hair. It was the
feel of her heavy hair in his hands, knowing no other man
had had the privilege or right to see her as he was seeing
her. It was the way she'd rested her forehead against his
shoulder, how she'd touched his face and hair as they lay
in each other's arms.

Somehow those moments had felt more intimate than
anything else. It made him ache in a way he didn't like,
opened up a deep well of yearning that had been dry and
empty for as long as he could remember.

Azim turned on the taps and washed his face, scrubbing
away that memory and the unsettling thoughts and feeling that came with it. So they had chemistry, undeniable

and overwhelming. That was good. It would serve them well in their marriage. That was all he needed to concern himself with now.

When he returned to the bedroom Johara had retrieved her nightgown and put it on, her cloud of dark hair hiding her face. She lay on her side, her back to him, her knees tucked up to her chest under the covers.

Azim hesitated, not wanting to prolong the moment but recognising just how innocent she'd been. 'You're all right?' he asked in a low voice. 'You're not…sore?'

She shook her head, her hair flying about her face, and before he could question or rethink the action Azim sat next to her and stroked her hair, tucking a few unruly tendrils behind her ear so he could see her face. The silvery tracks of tears shone on her cheeks. He drew his hand back, appalled.

'You said I didn't hurt you.'

'You didn't.' Her voice was muffled by the blankets she'd drawn up to her chin.

'Then why are you crying?' Azim demanded.

'I don't know.' Johara's voice sounded small, and she let out a hiccupy laugh. 'Isn't that silly?'

He didn't know if he would call it *silly*. He didn't like it, that was for certain. 'I do not appreciate a woman crying after I have made love to her,' he said, wincing inwardly at how cool he sounded. But he'd *felt* her passionate response. To cry afterwards was both idiotic and insulting.

'But we didn't make love, did we?' Johara pointed out. Azim stilled, even more appalled by her implication. She rolled onto her back to gaze at him openly, the tears still glistening on her cheeks.

'I know I'm being stupid,' she said. 'I know you don't love me. How could you? We barely know each other. And

I don't love you,' she added, which, infuriatingly, both re-assured and irritated him. 'I don't even want to.'

'Then what is the problem?' he asked in a clipped voice.

'I really don't know.' She sighed and swiped at her cheeks. 'I just feel sad for some reason.'

Impatient now, Azim rolled away from her. He couldn't deal with such emotional antics. Johara sighed softly, the sound one of weary resignation, and for a reason he could not fathom Azim felt compelled to say, his voice gruff, 'It is an emotional experience for any woman, I suppose.' It hadn't been for any of the women he'd slept with previously, but Johara was different—a virgin, innocent and naïve. *Hopeful.* Of course she would embroider romantic notions onto what they'd just done.

'Yes,' Johara agreed slowly. 'And it isn't for a man.'

'Not often.' Not ever, at least for him.

'Have you ever been in love?' she asked softly. 'Do you know what that feels like?'

'No.' The word was flat and uncompromising. As reluctant as he was to quash her completely, Azim knew what needed to be said. 'And I won't love you, Johara, if that is what you are hoping for. You are young and inexperienced, so it is natural perhaps for you to dream of romance. But you won't have it with me.'

'I wasn't asking,' she said with a spark that improbably made him smile. He was glad she hadn't lost her spirit.

'Good.'

'I've known that since you informed me we were going to marry,' Johara answered tartly. 'It was hardly a *romantic* proposal. And in any case, I don't want to love you. Why would I want to fall in love with someone who has no intention of loving me back?' Her voice was strident but also jagged, hiding pain. 'That's a recipe for disaster if there ever was one.'

'I'm pleased we're clear,' Azim returned, and they both lapsed into a tense silence. Azim rolled onto his back and stared at the ceiling; Johara turned back on her side, her back to him, her knees tucked up. He listened to her breathe, finding the gentle draw and tear strangely comforting. He had never actually slept with a woman before, the whole night through. Yet as tired as he was, it was an aggravatingly long time before he fell asleep.

Johara gave herself a stern talking-to when she readied and dressed the next morning. She and Azim had been woken up by attendants who had brought in a huge breakfast on a trolley of silver dishes and platters. A palace official had accompanied them, and Johara had blushed and retreated to the bathroom while he inspected the sheets for the needed proof of her virginity. Satisfied, he'd left them alone, as had the servants.

They'd eaten breakfast in bed, something that could have been romantic or even erotic but felt more like a business meeting.

'Your attendants will come shortly to take you back to the harem,' Azim said as he poured them both coffee.

'And that's where I stay?' She couldn't keep a note of ire and, worse, hurt from her voice.

'I am sure you will be entirely comfortable.'

Johara shook her head slowly. 'Am I really going to spend the rest of my life in a couple of rooms?'

'No, of course not. Why must you be so melodramatic?' Azim sounded irritated.

Johara lowered her coffee cup. 'I didn't realise I was being melodramatic.'

'You will accompany me on events around the city, and you will attend many dinners and other formal occasions in the palace. You are not a prisoner, Johara, and if you feel like you are, you do not know what real imprisonment feels like.'

Something about his tone made her ask, 'And you do?'

His expression closed, like a fan snapping shut. 'I know what it is to feel trapped.'

'How?'

He hesitated, and Johara held her breath waiting, hoping for more. 'The years after my kidnapping were not easy.' He took a sip of coffee, looking away, as if that was the end of the matter.

'You said they were unpleasant, but what do you mean by *trapped*?'

He pressed his lips together. 'It does not matter. I fought hard to survive and triumph, and I did. But there were years where I felt trapped, when there seemed no way out, no end to the suffering, and that experience was not like this.' With one impatient hand he gestured to their opulent surroundings, making Johara wince. It sounded as if he'd had a truly terrible experience, and here she was whingeing about all the luxury she was surrounded with.

'I'm sorry, Azim.'

He shrugged her words aside. 'This is not an imprisonment, Johara. You are free to do what you like in the women's quarters, to make friends among your attendants, to devote yourself to causes appropriate to your station. You have more freedom than most likely any other woman in Alazar.'

When he put it like that she felt petty and spoiled for complaining. And yet the life he was outlining still held a lack—a lack of companionship with her husband, a lack of friendship and, dared she think it, love. She'd told him last night that she didn't want love, but after what they'd done it was near impossible not to think of it. How could anyone not think of love when you gave your body, your whole self, so freely? It felt inconceivable to separate the two, and yet Azim obviously did, easily.

She'd been stupid to talk to him about love at all, Johara told herself as she returned to the harem to dress and ready for the day. What had she been expecting him to say? To do? Take her in his arms and whisper how much he cared, shower her with kisses and compliments? She was ridiculous for imagining that sex changed anything for him. She'd been pathetic, and that was one thing she did not intend to be again.

She had no wish to replicate the same kind of eager-to-please neediness she'd shown with her father. He'd only been kind to her when he'd wanted something, and in the bright, hard light of morning Johara recognised that Azim was essentially the same. Yes, he could give her lovely dresses and even lovelier kisses—but they cost him nothing. Nothing emotionally, anyway, which was what mattered.

And she was not going to fall in the trap of longing to love someone, *anyone*, who wouldn't love her back. *Love is a facile emotion.* No, she wouldn't give into it, or the desire for it.

Besides, she didn't even know Azim very well, although the more she knew, the more she realised how much he must have endured, how strong he was. The more she wanted to know him, and even now a little voice was whispering that perhaps if she was just patient, if she just waited for his hard heart to thaw, for him to learn to trust again, things could be different. He could love her, and she could love him, and it wouldn't be like her father said, facile, for fools and weaklings. Talk about being naïve.

Johara gazed at her reflection in exasperation. Pink cheeks, sparkling eyes, the look of a woman who had been thoroughly loved when she hadn't been. She'd been *en-*

joyed. Nothing emotional had happened last night, at least not for Azim.

And not, she determined, for her. From now on she was going to be like Azim, at least in his approach to their marriage. Briskly practical, enjoying the chemistry they obviously shared. Nothing more. Nothing that would make her feel hurt and used, and in a far worse way than she ever had with her father.

She spent the morning organising the women's quarters to her liking, getting rid of some of the fussy furniture and unpacking her own books and clothes and photographs, feeling better about having the space more personalised. At lunchtime she ate with Aisha and Basima, enjoying their friendly chatter.

In the afternoon she wandered out to the harem gardens, appreciating the pretty courtyard with its fountain and benches, and a larger terrace of landscaped shrubs and flowers. It was bigger than her garden back in France, and remembering what Azim had said, how much freedom she had, she turned to Aisha with a determined glint in her eye.

'Aisha, do you think you could bring me a spade?'

Azim spent the day in his office, meeting with Malik and other officials, trying to concentrate on the business at hand and finding it difficult. He kept thinking of Johara, reliving the best moments of their night together, and found himself so distracted he had to ask Malik to repeat things more than once.

'You must be tired,' Malik remarked with a mischievous glint in his eye, and Azim shook his head impatiently.

'I am fine.'

'It was your wedding night, brother. It is perfectly acceptable to admit to a little fatigue. Expected, I would have thought.' Malik spoke mildly, reminding Azim of the camaraderie they'd once had. If he hadn't been kidnapped, hardened beyond all bearing, he would have shared a laugh and a smile with his brother, and admitted to just how tired he was. Now he found he could not summon the tone, the lightness, but instead of his brother's remarks irritating him and putting him on the defensive, he found himself both frustrated and saddened by his own inability. He wanted more for himself, and yet he had no idea how to go about getting it. This wasn't a business deal or property transaction; he couldn't buy his way into deeper relationships. No, this was far more difficult, more confusing.

'I admit I am a bit tired,' he said stiffly, his best attempt at banter. 'But it is from the jet lag as much as anything else.'

A smile lurked in Malik's eyes as he sat down across from him to discuss their new policies for the country's tourism industry. 'Of course.'

By late afternoon Azim decided he'd had enough. He'd told himself he would not seek out Johara for the rest of the day, and only summon her to his chamber at night, as was befitting of a sultan-in-waiting and his new bride. He would not show he needed her, because he didn't, and such a gesture would smack of a weakness he could not show to the palace informants of the desert tribes, who were already suspicious of him for being too European, married to a woman who had spent most of her life in France.

Even so, after finishing a meeting with several diplomats, he excused himself from his study and found himself walking from the official front rooms and offices of the palace to the women's quarters at the back. He had not actually been to the harem since he was a boy, visiting his mother.

A memory, long forgotten, stirred, of his mother in the harem garden, watching goldfish dart through the still, cool waters of the pond, her slender, golden arm around his thin boy's shoulders. She'd died when he was six, and the harem had been closed and shuttered. Life had changed completely as his grandfather had taken over his upbringing, determined to weed out any weakness or sentiment, and Malik had been banished to the nursery and a host of nannies. His father, lost in grief, had become a shadow of a man, uninterested in either of his sons. And so for the next eight years Azim had learned to be sharp, to be quick, to be tough. And then he'd been kidnapped and he'd learned a whole new kind of tough.

'Your Highness!' A servant girl opened the door to the women's quarters, fluttering around him with girlish titters and blushes. 'If you are looking for Her Highness...'

'I am.'

'She is out in the garden.'

'Ah.' This was becoming something of a habit. His step grew lighter as he strode towards the louvred doors open to the enclosed gardens. He stopped on the threshold, arrested by the sight of his wife kneeling in a flower bed, her skirt caught up around her knees, digging with enthusiasm.

'We'll need another bag of compost before we can plant, Aisha,' she called. 'I wish we had some sort of irrigation or sprinkler system. Watering is going to be difficult.'

Quietly Azim closed the doors behind them, ensuring their privacy. 'I am afraid I am not Aisha.'

'Oh.' Startled, she turned around, her surprised expression morphing into wary pleasure as she smiled at him, her cheeks and eyes both glowing. 'I wasn't expecting to see you.'

'Were you not?'

She gave a little grimace. 'Basima told me you would only summon me at night.'

That had indeed been his plan, but now Azim shrugged it aside. 'I wanted to know how you were.'

A smile lit her face, lit up his insides. 'I'm well.'

'Busy.' He nodded towards the dug-up flowerbed. 'These gardens were prized, you know. The roses in particular.'

'Oh.' Her eyed widened in dismay. 'Were they? I should have asked, I suppose, but you did say I was free to do what I liked in here. I kept the rosebushes. I'm going to plant them on the other side.'

'I don't care about the roses,' he told her. 'I am glad to see you so occupied.' He was, fiercely so. He wanted her to make a life for herself here. He wanted, he realised, for her to be happy. 'You mentioned you had a garden in France?'

'Yes, mainly to grow herbs and plants for natural medicine.'

'Like the peppermint oil you used for my headache.'

'Yes.' Wanting to touch her, he took her hand and drew her up from the flowerbed to the bench by the fountain. 'You have dirt on your nose.' He brushed it off and she ducked her head.

'I must look a mess.'

'You look lovely. Enchanting.' Her hair was tucked up under a scarf, a few unruly tendrils escaping to frame her flushed face. He had the urge to kiss her, and so he did, brushing his lips once across hers, and then again, in a hello kiss that made him want to settle there, go deeper.

She drew back, searching his face, a frown developing between her brows.

'What is it?'

'Nothing.' She shook her head, smiling. 'I'm pleased to see you.'

'Good.' And then, to indulge himself, he kissed her again, taking the time to savour her sweetness, exploring the delectable softness of her mouth, tracing the seam of her lips with his tongue. The kiss went on, endless and aching, until Johara melted in his arms, her body pliant under his.

The sweetness of the kiss bred a deeper, more urgent need. Azim slid one hand under her skirt and Johara let out a breathy laugh.

'Someone will see…'

'The doors are shut, and your attendants know better than to disturb us. The walls are too high for anyone else to see.'

His fingers climbed higher, brushing her underwear, teasing her sensitive flesh, and Johara bit back a moan. He loved that he only had to touch her for her to start coming apart.

But then, with seeming superhuman effort, she batted his hand away. 'No.'

He stared at her in disbelief, battling a dismay and even hurt at her apparent rejection. 'No?'

Johara's eyes glittered as she answered with only a hint of shyness, 'If we are going to…well, then I want to touch you.'

Relief poured through him, along with something even sweeter. She wanted him. She wanted him as much as he wanted her. He sat back against the bench, his heart full, his body throbbing. 'Then by all means, go ahead.'

Johara glanced at Azim from beneath her lashes, his powerful body sprawled on the seat, muscular thighs spread, practically inviting her caress. She wondered if she'd issued a challenge she did not have the courage to carry out.

Last night she'd been a passive recipient, and, while it had certainly been pleasurable, now she wanted to take some control in this aspect of her life. She had so little control in others. And, she knew, she wanted to touch Azim. She wanted to see if he responded the same way to her touch as she did to his. She wanted to give him pleasure, to know she affected him at least in this.

Yet how…? Where to start?

'Surely you're not scared, Johara.' His voice was gently mocking, his lips curved in a small smile. He looked devastating sitting there, his eyes and hair so dark, his skin like burnished bronze, the crisp white shirt he wore highlighting the perfect musculature of his chest and abdomen.

'No.' She spoke with bravado and then, deciding she needed to dare, she placed one hand on his chest. Felt the steady thud of his heart under her palm, the muscles leap and jerk under her questing fingers, and a smile of pure feminine power curved her mouth. She could enjoy this.

Azim's dark eyes met with her own, and his mouth curved in an answering smile. 'That's a beginning.'

'Yes.' Not quite able to look at him, she focused on unbuttoning his shirt. Azim remained still under her clumsy movements—wretched buttons that didn't seem to want to come out of their holes. Then finally she'd got it unbuttoned, and she spread the shirt so she had a full view of his chest.

He was truly glorious, his skin taut over sculpted muscles, a sprinkling of dark hair veeing down to his trousers. She trailed her fingertips down his bare skin, from his throat to his belly button, and her blood heated at the hot look of naked need in Azim's eyes.

'All you have to do is touch me to make me want you.' She trailed her fingers back up and he leaned his head against the bench, closing his eyes. 'You don't even have to touch me. All it takes is a look, a thought, and I'm yours.'

Yours. She wanted him to be hers. If she was honest

with herself, she wanted him to be hers more than in this, but she'd take this for now. She'd revel in it.

In one purposeful movement she slid onto his lap, lifting her skirt up to her hips so she could straddle his thighs.

Azim's eyes gleamed and colour appeared on his high cheekbones. She could feel his arousal pressing against her, and remembered when he'd brought her onto his lap before. When he'd touched her most intimately. Now it was her turn.

'I think I like this,' he murmured.

Now the brazen part. She tugged at the zip of his trousers, gasping a little at the feel of his arousal pressing so insistently against her hand. Then she freed him, and dared to stroke his full length, amazed at her own courage, the feel of his hot, satiny skin under her fingertips.

'Yes, I like this very much,' Azim murmured, his breath hissing between his teeth, his voice a husky growl of need. 'But make sure you finish what you started.'

Finish... Realisation dawned, and, with it, power. She could do this. She would do this, because the knowledge that Azim wanted her as much as she wanted him was heady and empowering. 'I intend to,' she said, and then she rose up on her knees and, pushing her clothing aside, sank slowly onto him, sheathing him inside her. *'Oh.'* She gasped as new sensations hit her synapses. 'It feels different than before.'

He laughed, the sound low and throaty as his hips began to move against hers. 'Different good?'

'Yes.' She was starting to lose the power of speech, her mind going blissfully blank as she matched his movements. 'Yes, definitely. *Definitely.*'

Later, after they'd tidied themselves up and Azim rang for refreshments, Johara marvelled at her audacity. Sitting in the sunshine with Azim's arm around her shoulders, she thought she was the happiest she'd been in a long time. The fact that he'd come to find her was like a song in her heart, a secret she hugged to herself, promising more. Never mind her resolutions of that morning; they'd scattered away with the first breath of hope. She didn't want to live like her father. She didn't want to guard her heart and stay isolated and alone, as Azim had been for so long. She wanted more, even if it hurt. Even if it meant risk of pain. Wasn't that what true optimism, true hope, was all about? And right now she felt more hopeful than ever that in time Azim could begin to care for her. Just as she could—and was already doing.

'Why natural medicine?' he asked as he toyed with a tendril of her hair. They were sitting together on the bench, sipping mint tea that Aisha had brought. Johara thought she'd detected a mischievous, knowing glint in the young girl's eye and wondered if her attendant had guessed what they'd been up to.

'Our cook, Lucille, introduced me to herbal remedies when I was trying to alleviate my mother's worst symptoms. I started a garden with her help and began to read books about it.'

'Did they work on your mother?'

'Sometimes.' Johara paused, not-so-pleasant memories invading and darkening the sunshine of the afternoon. 'She had terrible headaches, which is why I recognised when you had one. And she also was…lethargic.' Which was putting it mildly.

'Do you know what caused it?'

Johara hesitated, feeling that they were on shaky ground. 'My father never loved her,' she began slowly. 'Or so she told me.' As a girl she realised now how thoughtlessly she'd dismissed her mother's complaints, because she'd adored her father and could sympathise with why he'd lost patience with his sad and listless wife. But now she experienced a sharp pang of sympathy for her mother. To live without love was a terrible thing. To endure each day, knowing it promised no happiness, no hope. It made her insides quail with fear for the path she'd now chosen. What if Azim never came to care for her? What if she fell in love with him and ended up like her mother? It was, perhaps, more risk than she wanted to take and yet the alternative was awful. A cold, lonely existence of always guarding her heart, watching her step.

'And she'd loved him?' Azim's voice gave nothing away, but Johara could feel how his body had tensed against her.

'Yes, at least she said she did. But she also miscarried several times. The lack of children was a great disappointment to both of them, and especially not having a son.' She wrinkled her nose, tried for a little laugh, to lighten the mood. She knew Azim didn't like talking about love, and it made her a little uncomfortable too. 'I'm afraid I wasn't a great consolation prize.'

Azim's fingers brushed her cheek. 'You are a great prize to me.'

Johara's throat thickened with emotion. She didn't doubt Azim's sincerity, and her heart rejoiced at him saying even this much, for it was more than anything he'd said before, and yet…

She didn't want to be a prize. She wanted to be a partner. A lover, a soul mate, his heart's desire. The realisation bloomed and grew within her like the most fragrant and beautiful flower in any garden. She was, slowly and inexorably, falling in love with her husband—and she wanted, quite desperately, for him to love her back. The possibility that he might never do so was enough to freeze the smile on her face, everything in her aching with both hope—and fear.

CHAPTER THIRTEEN

'WE ARE TRAVELLING to Najabi.'

Azim stood in the doorway of her stillroom, looking alarmingly grave. Johara's heart tumbled in her chest, as it had a habit of doing every time she caught sight of her husband. They had been married for three weeks and, while it felt like no time at all, it also seemed as if things had been this way for ever.

They'd fallen into a sweet pattern that Johara treasured; she worked in her garden most mornings and she usually saw Azim in the afternoon, when he stopped by the women's quarters for a visit. They ate dinner together most nights and she'd spent every night in his bed.

It was more, far more, than she'd ever expected to have in this forced marriage, and yet in the quiet stillness of her own heart she knew she wanted still more. She wanted Azim's love, and she didn't have it yet. He was attentive, yes, and a most exciting and ingenious lover, if a little remote, often rolling off the bed and dressing the moment they'd finished.

They had developed a rapport of conversation, discussing ideas, politics, art, almost anything but themselves. At least, Azim did not discuss himself, and Johara had learned not to ask. The information he shared about himself and his past came in reluctant, tersely given snippets, and she treasured each precious new fact, few as they were.

The day after he'd visited her in her makeshift garden, Azim had sent a raft of new garden supplies and two able-bodied attendants to help her transform the garden's pruned perfection into the kind of wild and unruly sanctuary she'd had in France. He'd also arranged for one of the rooms of her quarters to be turned into a stillroom, complete with a deep, stone sink and a stove for preparing and distilling essential oils and making salves.

His thoughtfulness had both touched her and given her hope, and she'd spent many happy hours tending her garden and preparing her medicines. Word of her prowess had reached many of the occupants of the palace, and many days she was treating an attendant or official for some minor complaint or ailment. She'd gone to two state dinners, and had started to get to know Malik's fiancée Gracie before she'd returned to America to prepare for a final move to Alazar.

All of it gave her a sense of purpose and community, both of which she realised had been missing from her previous life.

'Najabi?' she asked now, her heart tripping at how solemn Azim looked. 'Where is that?'

'In the desert. I need to visit the desert tribes and assure them of my loyalty to both them and their traditions.'

'Which is where I come in,' Johara surmised. 'I need to play the dutiful bride?'

'You are a dutiful bride,' Azim replied with the flicker of a smile. 'But yes. It will reassure them to know that my bride is not corrupting me, and that I have her firmly under control.' He spoke lightly, almost joking, but Johara knew he was serious. And as excited as she would be for a trip with Azim, she wasn't looking forward to them playing these assumed roles. At least, she hoped they were assumed. She hoped they'd come a long way from the marriage of cold convenience they'd once had.

'When do we leave?'

'Tomorrow, for a few days. We will visit several different tribes. They are planning some celebrations for us. It will be hard travel, though,' he warned. 'The interior of Alazar is rugged, with few roads. Basima will help you pack appropriately.'

'And when we're there?' Johara asked with a touch of apprehension. 'What will I do? How am I supposed to be?'

'You can take your cue from me,' Azim said, which didn't help all that much. 'This is important, Johara,' he added, his tone grave. 'For us, and for Alazar.'

The next day they took a helicopter for the hundreds of miles into Alazar's interior, a barren, rock-strewn landscape of endless desert, the mountains of Alazar's impressive ranges piercing the horizon.

Johara spent most of the time gazing out of the window, marvelling at the stunning scenery and trying not to feel sick with nerves. Since they'd started this trip Azim had retreated into a tense silence that reminded her so much of the first days of their marriage, when they had been like strangers, and hostile ones at that.

She'd thought they had got past those early, awful days, but maybe they hadn't. The trouble was, she had no idea how strong their marriage really was, how real their bond. At times, when Azim was smiling at something she'd said or holding her in his arms, stroking her hair or moving inside her, she felt as if they were both on the cusp of everything. Of love.

But in a moment like this one she felt as if she was being ridiculous, reading emotion and feeling where there was none. She was being pathetic and needy, grasping at whatever Azim tossed her way, and she never wanted to be either again.

'Why aren't we taking a helicopter directly to where we're going?' she asked. Azim had already told her that they would land several hours away from the first tribe's encampment.

'Because as their leader it would be shaming to do so,' Azim explained. 'It would seem weak and unmanly.'

She shook her head slowly. 'And riding in an SUV doesn't?'

Azim gave her a ghost of a smile. 'We are not riding in an SUV.'

'But how are we getting there, then?'

'Horseback.'

'Horseback!' She stared at him, appalled. 'I've never been on a horse before in my life.'

'Something which will be remedied shortly.' Azim's expression remained unsmiling, not so much as a flicker of a smile to soften it. 'You will ride with me.'

He had never been into Alazar's arid heart before. His preparation for the Sultanate had been a life in Teruk and then the start of military school. Asad would have taken him into the desert eventually, Azim supposed, but he felt the absence of experience now.

He shielded his eyes with one hand from the relentless desert sun as Johara climbed out of the helicopter behind him. They were several hours' ride from the first encampment, in a bleak moonscape of undulating sand strewn with large, fearsome-looking rocks. A groom waited with their horses and supplies, brought from an outpost nearby.

Azim thanked him as he took the reins of his horse. He felt on edge, wound too tight, the first flickers of a head-

ache pulsing through his brain. His conversation with his
grandfather yesterday still ricocheted unpleasantly through
him.

'She is making a fool of you.'

Azim had stared at the old man now confined to his
bed, bitter and alone, and tried not to react. Asad struggled
up to a sitting positon, his claw-like hands grasping the
sheets, his breath coming in desperate wheezes. The doctor had given him a few months to live, if that, and when
Azim had heard the news he'd felt nothing.

Once he'd felt something for the old man. He'd glowed
under his tersely given praise, had sought to please him by
working hard, by being tough. In the twenty years since
his kidnapping he'd forgotten Asad completely, forgotten
Alazar. But seeing his grandfather's face on the television
had brought it all back, and the first emotion that had hit
him in the face had been fury. A deep-seated rage at this
man who had ridden him so hard, yielding no quarter or
kindness. Now he eyed him coldly, refusing to rise to the
obvious bait.

'I am travelling to Alazar's interior tomorrow.'

'Did you not hear what I said?'

'Yes, I simply chose not to respond to it.'

'People are talking. Whispers about how she spends
every night in your bed.'

'I want an heir,' Azim stated flatly.

'And you go to the harem, almost every day.' Asad's
voice was a hiss of disbelief. 'You are besotted with her
paltry charms.' Azim said nothing, a muscle ticcing in his
jaw. 'What do you think the desert tribes will say?' Asad
rasped. 'They will think you are controlled by a woman,
and a European one at that.'

'Johara was the country's choice,' Azim returned. 'Her

blood is nearly as noble as ours. She has been destined for the throne as much as I am.'

'But she has not lived it,' Asad pointed out. 'Just as you haven't. Tucked away in France as she's been... People wonder, and you are making it worse.'

'Is that all?' Azim asked coldly. 'I have business to attend to.' He turned away without waiting for his grandfather's reply.

'People say you are like him, Azim,' Asad wheezed after him. 'Like your father.'

Azim slammed the door behind him.

Now he straddled the stallion that had been brought for him and tried to banish his grandfather's words from his mind. He was not like his father. He was not weak. Not any longer. He'd spent far too long being virtually helpless, at another's mercy, and he'd lived his life in a decidedly different fashion since. Yes, he enjoyed Johara's company—and her body. That wasn't wrong. It didn't have to be weakness. But he couldn't get his grandfather's words out of his head, and that irritated him.

'I didn't realise horses were so big.' Johara glanced up at him, swathed from head to foot in a linen robe both for modesty and protection from the desert heat and blowing sand.

'The groom will help you up.' Azim looked away, ignoring the flicker of hurt he'd seen pass across his bride's face. He'd been short with her since the conversation he'd had with his grandfather; he hadn't summoned her last night or spoken to her much on their travels here.

He felt a pang of guilt for hurting her, but he told himself it was necessary. Perhaps they both needed to be reminded of the parameters of their relationship. Perhaps he had been too indulgent, both of her and his own whims.

Then they would be able to move on in a way that was beneficial for them both.

The groom helped Johara up and with a muffled *oof* she sprawled across the horse, her breasts pressed against his thighs. She glanced up at him wryly, challenging him to see the humour in the situation, but Azim just took her arm and hauled her up to a sitting position, her back against his chest.

He wrapped one arm around her middle, under her breasts, and clicked to the horse. They started off, jolting across the sand, and Johara settled into him more closely. Azim tried not to react to the feel of her against him, the rightness of having her body pressed against his.

As the horse began to gallop, the wind streaming past them, he felt a sudden surge of primal, possessive power, an overwhelming sense that Johara was *his*—his to care for and to protect. To love. The word popped into his head and he quickly banished it. He couldn't think that way. Love was weakness. Trust was stupidity. He *knew* that. He'd seen it too many times—first with his father, and then with Caivano. Trusting someone meant giving them power. Loving them meant risking pain and betrayal.

His arm tightened around her middle and she looked up at him, a frown between her brows, a question in her eyes. Azim looked away from her gaze, at the stretch of sand in front of them, and rode on.

By the time they arrived at the Najabi oasis his body was aching from the hard ride, and he could only imagine how much Johara, who had never ridden before, felt. She had not complained once, though, and for that Azim felt more than a flicker of admiration. His wife was strong.

Now they approached the oasis, the leaders of the tribe assembled to welcome them. The moment felt taut with suppressed tension, suspicion and vague hostility. Johara had dropped behind him, her head modestly lowered, meeting no one's gaze just as she was meant to. What would have filled him with satisfaction and relief now he found irritated and even troubled him.

He didn't want Johara behind him like some lackey. He wanted her at his side, raising her face, smiling at everyone as he announced her as his bride. The urge to reach for her, to bring her forward, was almost overwhelming, and Azim didn't know whether to feel appalled or proud. Where had this feeling come from? The strength of it was surprising, disturbing. He nodded towards one of the leaders, who, after an endless moment, made his obeisance. And still he thought of Johara.

Johara could feel the suppressed male energy and hostility shimmering in the desert heat as several leaders bowed to Azim, their expressions stoic and grim. She'd kept her head lowered but she couldn't resist peeking up to see what was going on.

The silence stretched on, the only sound the wind starting to kick up. A horse nickered. Then, like a gunshot, a sudden eruption of chatter and laughter started. Johara raised her head, startled, and saw a bevy of women in brightly coloured hijabs and robes coming towards her, their faces wreathed in welcoming smiles.

The men, seeming to take their cue from the women, slapped Azim on the back and welcomed him into their fold. With relief she realised that the tense moment of uncertainty had passed.

The women enveloped her, pulling her along, and with one last startled look for Azim, Johara let herself be led away.

The women took her to a tent, chattering all the while, giving her nudges and winks as they remarked on what a handsome man the Sultan-to-be was, and then burst into uproarious laughter. Johara soon found herself caught up in the mood, laughing and chatting with them, even daring to make a few ribald jokes, which the women loved, although her heart still felt heavy.

Why was Azim being so cold? They'd spent hours riding together, and yet Johara felt as if she might as well have been a sack of potatoes he had to haul around. She didn't understand his withdrawal, or what prompted this sudden coolness. Was it simply a concern for the desert tribes—or something deeper and more alarming? Perhaps this was simply a reflection of his true feelings—or lack of them.

After plying her with glasses of cool *sharbat* and honey cakes, the women led her out to a sheltered spot in the oasis where they bathed, insisting Johara join in.

After several aching hours in the saddle, she was more than glad to wash off the sand and dust of travel, even if she felt a little shy stripping down. The women gave her a new robe to wear, of cream linen embroidered with purple and gold, fit for a princess.

Johara realised a meal was being prepared for her and Azim, a celebration for the Sultan-to-be and his bride. Her heart seemed to miss a beat as the women led her out to the circle of waiting men, who nodded in approval to see her so traditionally dressed. Johara peeked through the gauzy veil, looking for the only man whose opinion mattered. But when she finally caught sight of Azim, his face was expressionless, and when her eyes met his he looked away.

What was going on?

The evening passed in a miserable blur, although Johara tried to smile and laugh and chat for the women's benefit. She was confused and angry with Azim for being so remote, and cross with herself for caring. She had not followed her own directive at all, which was to stay calm and cool and in control, to be as remote as Azim was when it came to their relationship.

No, she'd done exactly what she hadn't wanted to do—been lured in by a few paltry presents and kindnesses, things that cost Azim nothing. And she'd built it up in her head, in her heart. She'd pretended it was enough, that it was something on the way to love.

After the celebrations Johara readied for bed in the tent provided for her and Azim. With the throw pillows and fresh, fragrant herbs scattered around, the flickering candlelight, it was the epitome of desert romance—and utterly wasted, as Azim was ensconced with the leaders of the tribe and did not look to be coming to bed any time soon.

It took her a long time to fall asleep, listening to the horses nickering softly, the wind rustling the sides of the tent. Eventually she dropped off, stirring only when Azim came into the tent. She rolled over, wanting to welcome him, but he simply took off his outer robe and lay a few feet apart from her, his back to her. With her heart like a stone, Johara fell asleep again.

She woke some time in the night, startling awake although she didn't know why—until she saw the empty expanse of sleeping mat next to her. Azim had gone.

Johara lay there for a few moments, undecided, before in one swift movement she rose from the mat, grabbing her robe and pulling it on over her nightgown. Then, having no idea where she was going, she slipped out of the tent in search of her husband.

The desert felt eerily silent and still as she moved through the camp like a shadow. Moonlight spilled on the sand like silver, illuminating the cluster of horses, the round, humped shapes of the tents. If Azim was in the camp, it wasn't obvious.

Guided more by instinct than anything else, Johara left

the tents for the oasis a short walk away, now glimmering like a smooth, silver plate under the moonlight. It was perfectly still and completely empty. She started to turn away when she heard the soft sound of splashing, and realised Azim had to be bathing in the sheltered spot of the oasis where she had been with the women earlier.

Tiptoeing now, her heart slamming in her chest, she crept around a stand of date palms to the small inlet where the women had bathed.

She saw his head first, then arms and a muscled torso cutting through the calm water like dark silk. He moved with sinuous grace and purpose, and Johara simply stood, admiring his perfect form, when Azim rose from the water like a selkie emerging from the waves, water sluicing from him and running in rivulets down his gleaming body.

A shaft of moonlight fell over him in a ribbon of silver, illuminating his muscled back—and Johara gasped out loud.

Azim stilled and then slowly turned. His expression, visible in the moonlit darkness, was one of terrible, ominous neutrality.

'What the hell are you doing here?'

CHAPTER FOURTEEN

SHE'D SEEN HIS SCARS. No one saw those, that shame. Azim had always made sure of it. He never changed in public, never presented his back to a lover, never gave anyone at all an opportunity to see those terrible marks of his servitude.

Since his marriage to Johara he'd made sure to keep his back away from her and dress as quickly as possible. It was the one thing above all the others that he'd wanted to keep secret. Judging from the horror and pity marking her face, Johara had just seen every wretched scar and knew what he'd allowed himself to be subjected to.

'How did it happen?' Johara asked in an appalled whisper.

Azim strode out of the water and grabbed his shirt, pulling it on roughly. Johara stretched out one hand.

'Azim...'

'I was beaten,' he said flatly. 'Like a dog. What else?'

'But who—?'

He shook his head, the movement abrupt, impatient. He was filled with a fury he didn't fully understand. Was he angry at Johara, for seeing something she shouldn't have, or himself, for letting it happen, for having the scars all? Or Caivano, whom he'd long ago destroyed, for what he'd done?

'Was it from the kidnapping?' Johara asked quietly. 'When they beat you?'

It would be so easy to lie and say yes, it was. Yes, his unknown kidnappers had marked his back as well as his face, had left him a bloody pulp in an alleyway in Naples. Wouldn't that be simple? Understandable, at least. But he couldn't make himself lie. Not about this.

'No.' The word was choked through a throat that suddenly felt like a vice.

'Then when? Not your grandfather?'

'No.' He let out a harsh laugh. 'My grandfather can be cruel, but he would never have marked me like that. Someone of royal blood shouldn't...' He stopped, because for some reason he could no longer squeeze the words out. *No real man allows himself to be beaten. Used.* As he had.

'Oh, Azim.'

'Don't pity me.' His word was the savage crack of a whip. 'I can stand just about anything but that.'

'I don't pity you,' Johara said quietly. 'But I am sorry for what you have endured. Why won't you tell me, though? I want to understand you, Azim. I want to know—'

'Fine, you want to know?' His voice was a harsh grating in his own ears. 'The man who rescued me from the hospital, who claimed he knew me, that he was a beloved uncle, the man who told me my name was Rafael Olivieri—he was lying. All of it utter lies. He saw a vulnerable boy, someone with no resources or friends. He saw a slave.'

Even now, twenty years later, the memory had the power to leave him breathless with shame and worse, hurt. He'd been so *grateful* to Caivano, had considered him like a father for the weeks he'd been in the hospital. Caivano had played along, bringing him presents, luring him in. And in response Azim, a lonely, hurting boy, had loved him. His captor.

'What happened…?' Johara asked, her eyes wide and round with the horror of it.

'He brought me back to his garage and forced me to work there without pay, like a slave. When I tried to escape, this happened.' He gestured to his back.

Johara's face was pale, her jaw slack. He'd shocked her. Horrified her. And Azim wished he hadn't told her, because how could she look at him the same again? She'd always see the scars, and remember how he'd got them. She'd see a victim rather than a man.

'How did you finally escape?' she asked in a whisper.

'It took a long time. Caivano was a Mafioso. He had friends in ugly places, which meant it was nearly impossible to get away. It was four years before I was able to figure out a plan.' He drew a breath, his chest hurting, the blood rushing in his ears. 'I got him drunk and found evidence of his crimes. I blackmailed him into giving me my freedom, and I used money I'd stolen from him to make my first property deal. And I always watched my back.'

'What happened to him? This man?' Johara asked.

'I ruined him.' He spoke flatly, without emotion. For ten years he'd slept with a knife under his pillow, one eye cracked open, always on alert. When he'd finally been able to ruin Caivano six years ago, the revenge had been ice-cold but still sweet, even if it had left him wanting more. Craving more validation for who he was, what he'd become.

'Ruined him? How?'

'I bought out his business and then destroyed it. It took me ten years but he had to declare bankruptcy, a broken man. My villa in Naples used to belong to him. I bought it for a song when he had nothing left.'

Johara's face twisted in a grimace Azim couldn't decipher. 'Did that make you feel better?'

'Yes, as a matter of fact, it did.' But not good enough. No matter who he destroyed, he still felt empty inside. Azim had no intention of saying any of that to his wife. 'I waited a long time for revenge.'

'I suppose I can understand that,' she said sadly. 'If it helped you to heal…'

'I didn't need to *heal*,' Azim said, his mouth twisting. 'I needed to right a wrong.' He pulled on his trousers and turned his back on her. 'Go back to the tent, Johara.' He waited a few seconds but she didn't move. The seconds ticked by, each one taut with pain and grief. 'Why are you still here?' he demanded.

'Why are you being so cold with me?' Johara threw back. 'Ever since you told me we were going to Najabi you have been more and more remote. We were getting along, Azim. At least I thought we were. But now I realise just how little you've told me. Shown me.'

His fists clenched. 'I've never shown anyone my scars.'

'But I am your *wife*. Were you going to keep your back from me for ever? I always wondered why you never let me hold you when we were making love. Why you dressed so quickly afterwards. But it couldn't have gone on for ever, surely? I would have seen some time. And then what would have happened?'

He didn't answer. What could he say? It sounded ridiculous, pathetic, to hide from his own wife, and yet all he knew was that he couldn't let someone see what he'd allowed to be done to him. He couldn't reveal that kind of weakness, see it in her eyes, feel the pity.

'I don't understand you,' she said in a soft, sad voice. 'I thought I was beginning to, I thought we were starting to…'

'I warned you, Johara.' His voice rang out in the still-ness. 'I always warned you. This was never going to be the fairy-tale romance you seemed intent on it being. There is only one thing between us. This.'

Azim's hands came down hard on Johara's shoulders and then he was pulling her towards him, his mouth crashing down onto hers. What was meant to be a cruel reminder, a punishment even, still had the power to spark her soul and make heat pool in her belly. She wasn't going to let him turn their lovemaking into something angry or venge-ful. Not as everything else in his life seemed to have been.

Johara reached up and wrapped her arms around Azim's neck, pressing her body into his, the damp linen of his shirt wetting her robe, moulding them together. Her mouth opened under his as she deepened and gentled the kiss.

Azim let out a harsh cry, and Johara didn't know if she'd made him angrier or she'd finally caused a crack in the iron shell her husband had surrounded himself with for so long.

They stumbled backwards, mouths still locked in a battle for punishment or tenderness, passion blazing with darkness and fire. Still kissing, they fell onto the sand, limbs tangling, hands reaching, everything urgent and desperate.

Azim pulled at her robe, yanking it up to her waist, his hands skimming her secret places, fingers probing, know-ing exactly what made her melt and want.

Damp heat licked her insides as she opened herself to him, accepted every angry caress and asked for more. He would not win this battle. She would be triumphant in seeming defeat.

With a harsh cry Azim drove into her and Johara ac-cepted him, wrapping her legs around his waist, drawing him in even more deeply, their bodies moving in urgent rhythm, searching for that desperate pleasure.

Johara slid her hands up under his shirt, holding on even as Azim tried to shrug her off, and she smoothed her palms across the deep ridges that criss-crossed his back, so many of them, and each one broke her heart. She could not imagine how Azim had endured such a thing, a young boy bent on his freedom, a near-man determined to be strong and proud. She touched each one with gentle, soothing fingertips, willing him to accept her caress, to feel the love that she was offering him freely with every touch, wanting to imbue him with the strength she felt.

Pleasure pierced her with its sharp sweetness as their bodies moved in sync, reaching for that shimmering apex. Then everything splintered into sensation-sated fragments and with a groan Azim relaxed on top of her, his body shuddering in the aftermath of their shared climax. Neither of them spoke.

Eventually he rolled off her, lying on his back, one arm thrown over his face. Johara blinked up at him, tears thickening her throat. She'd been shocked by the scars on his back, and hurt by the fury he'd shown, dismayed by the savage satisfaction she'd heard in his voice when he'd told her about ruining that man, and yet over all of it, stronger than ever, was a deep, aching love.

Watching him lie there now, she saw a man who had been pushed beyond all endurance, who had been broken and bound himself together again. A man who was incredibly strong. A man she loved.

'Azim…' she began, wanting to tell him something of what was in her heart, but Azim shook his head wordlessly. She rolled closer and saw, to her shock, a tear gleaming on one stubbled cheek. *'Azim.'* She reached for his hand. 'Don't shut me out now, please. Not because of this.'

He didn't speak for a long moment, his arm still covering his eyes. 'I can't stand the thought of you knowing. Thinking of me that way.'

'What way?' Johara cried. Azim didn't reply and realisation dawned slowly, a creeping mist. 'Azim, do you think I'd believe you to be *weak*, because of that? Because some evil, sick man beat you when you were young and vulnerable?'

'I wasn't that young,' he answered in a low voice. 'I was strong enough to have overpowered him if I'd wanted to.'

'Then why didn't you?' Johara challenged. 'If you could?'

He shook his head briefly, his eyes closed. 'Azim?' Johara pressed, sensing this was important. 'Why didn't you?'

'Because I was scared.' His voice was a barely audible whisper. 'As scared as a small, stupid child. Of Caivano and the power I knew he had. And also because…because there was a part of me…' He broke off, shaking his head again, and Johara waited, her breath held. 'I hated him,' Azim said slowly. 'I hated him so much. And yet he was the only person I knew. The only person who meant anything to me. I think I was afraid to let go of that, even as I dreamed of freedom. Yearned for it with every breath in my body.' He let out a shudder and tried to turn away from her, but Johara wouldn't let him.

'You are the strongest person I know, Azim,' she said steadily, wrapping her arms around him, refusing to let him go. 'For enduring so much and not just surviving, but triumphing. Look at the business you built up on your own. Look at the kingdom you are determined to rule, bound by your honour and duty. You're strong.' She held on and, after an endless moment, Azim put his arms around her.

They lay on the cool, damp sand, their arms around one another, neither of them speaking, for a long moment. And then Azim murmured two words, words Johara knew came from deep within him.

'Thank you.'

CHAPTER FIFTEEN

THEY SPENT THE next few days travelling from tribe to tribe, greeting, discussing, celebrating. At night Azim always reached for her, and Johara went joyfully. She had no idea what was going on behind her husband's inscrutable expression, but she felt they were going forward. She had to believe that. She longed to tell Azim she loved him, but somehow the moment was never right.

At night they barely spoke, communicating with their bodies, and during the day they were constantly surrounded by tribespeople, except when travelling, and galloping on a horse wasn't conducive to deep conversation.

When they got back to Teruk, Johara promised herself. Then she'd tell him what was in her heart…and perhaps he would as well.

Yet the moment the helicopter touched down Azim was striding away, leaving Johara to make her own way to the harem. She watched his retreating figure and tried to hold onto hope. He was a sultan in training, she reminded herself, and virtually running the country by himself since his grandfather was ill and bedridden. He was busy. He'd find her later, and then they'd talk.

But he didn't. Johara busied herself in her quarters, trying not to mind, not to panic. With each passing hour that Azim stayed away she felt her hopes flag and then plummet. A day passed, and then another, and Azim did not contact her at all.

Late in the afternoon two days after Johara had arrived back from the desert, she received an unexpected visitor—Gracie, Malik's fiancée. Johara had met her only briefly before she'd gone back to America, and seeing her again, looking so relaxed and friendly, clearly confident in Malik's love, made Johara feel both shy and envious.

'How are you settling in?' Gracie asked after Aisha had brought them almond and honey pastries and tea in the garden. 'It looks as if you've made this place your own. I remember these gardens as having far more shrubbery.'

'You stayed here?' Johara exclaimed in surprise.

'Briefly, when I first came here with Sam.' She made a face. 'I don't know how much you've heard…'

'I haven't heard anything.'

'I met Malik briefly a long time ago,' Gracie explained. 'And then had Sam, his son.' She grimaced again. 'I know what it sounds like, but…'

'Trust me, I do not judge.' Johara was just grateful *someone* was being candid and open with her.

'Anyway,' Gracie resumed with a grateful smile, 'we… reconnected a little while ago, and then we got engaged. It all happened fast—'

'Surely not as fast as my own marriage,' Johara interjected with a wry grimace. 'I met Azim only days before we wed.'

'It's hard, isn't it?' Gracie said softly, and Johara feared she saw too much in her face.

'It is hard,' she agreed slowly, trying not to reveal a tremor of uncertainty in her voice, 'but it doesn't always have to be, I hope.'

Gracie nodded slowly. 'Malik said you and Azim had been getting along well…?'

'I thought we were. But Azim…' Johara paused, not wanting to reveal any of Azim's secrets, knowing how precious they were. 'I don't think he expected us to have a real relationship,' she finally explained. 'A loving one.'

'Neither did Malik.' Gracie shook her head. 'These Bahjat men. They haven't had it easy, but they don't make it easy for us, either.'

Johara smiled at that, even though her heart still felt weighed down by sadness. 'No,' she agreed. 'They don't.'

It was two days since he'd seen Johara. Two endless days, and yet Azim still stayed away. After everything she'd seen, all that he'd shared, he was afraid to see her again. Talk properly, alone, and have their relationship deepen or be destroyed—he didn't know which. Did she pity him? Could he feel more for her, if he let himself? Did he even want to? They were all questions that tormented him and had no answers, and so he avoided her. Maybe it was a cowardly way out, but it felt like the only option now. He was too unsure, too damned raw, for anything else.

There was a state banquet that night to welcome European leaders, and he'd sent her a message to prepare for it. He found that, against all his apprehension, he was still looking forward to seeing her, maybe too much. And yet he also welcomed the leap of excitement he felt in his belly as he waited for her in one of the palace's private salons. He needed to touch her, to look into her face and see—what? What if he saw pity or worse? Azim swore under his breath, folding his arms and setting his jaw. He had to stop thinking this way.

The doors creaked open, and Azim turned, his heart tumbling in his chest at the sight of Johara. She wore an evening gown of deep cerise that cinched her waist and flared out in gauzy swirls about her slender legs. Her hair was piled on top of her head, and diamonds winked at her ears and throat. She looked magnificent.

The smile she gave him managed to be both tremulous and tart. 'Long time no see.'

He prickled, already on the defensive, still feeling far too exposed. 'I've been busy.'

'Of course.' She held her head high, her eyes glittering. 'Shall we?'

Azim hesitated, not wanting to start the evening with an argument. He understood why she was hurt, and yet he struggled to verbalise it. Half of him was insisting it was better this way, and the other half… 'I'm sorry,' he said abruptly. Johara arched an eyebrow.

'For what?'

'Not coming to see you.'

She shrugged her slender shoulders, her gaze sliding away. 'You said you were busy.'

She was hiding her hurt, a form of self-defence he understood all too well.

'Not that busy. The truth is…' Azim took a breath and blew it out. 'I haven't known what to say to you.'

Her wide, silvery gaze flew to his. 'What do you mean?'

'I feel like I told you too much.' He looked away, hating that he'd said even that.

'Azim…' Johara laid a hand on his arm, her touch gentle and yet still inflaming. An attendant knocked on the doors of the salon.

'We need to go.' Azim placed his hand over hers, his jaw set. He didn't want to talk about this now. He couldn't.

He saw resignation douse the hope in her eyes as she slowly nodded. 'All right.'

All evening long he was conscious of her on his arm, her friendly smile, the easy way she chatted with world leaders, treating everyone the same—as a potential friend.

She was lovely and warm and entirely genuine, and it made his heart both surge and contract. She made him feel, she woke him up, and the knowledge was terrifying. What was he going to do with it?

Towards the end of the evening Malik appeared by his elbow. 'There is something you need to see.'

Azim tensed at the urgent note of command in his brother's voice. 'Now?'

'Yes. Now.'

Azim made his excuses to the various dignitaries he'd been with and followed Malik to his office. 'This better be important.'

'It is.' Malik's face was grim as he took a paper from his breast pocket and handed it to Azim. 'One of our ambassadors sent me a scan of this just now. It hits the European tabloids tomorrow.'

Frowning, Azim glanced down at the paper—and then froze as he took in the headline. *Future Sultan of Alazar Once Held As A Slave and Beaten.* His jaw tight, his blood beating hard through his veins, he read the entire article, inwardly flinching at every terrible word that described his imprisonment with 'a nameless Mafioso', the beatings he'd endured, the failed escapes. The reporter knew everything. *Everything he'd told Johara...and no one else.*

'I'm so sorry, Azim.' Malik's voice was choked. 'I had no idea you'd endured so much.'

Azim tossed the paper aside. 'It doesn't matter.'

'It does—'

'No.' His voice came out like the crack of a gunshot. 'It doesn't.' He took a deep, steadying breath. Could Johara really have told a reporter about him? Sold his story—and for what? Money? Revenge?

He couldn't believe it, didn't want to, and yet...he'd been betrayed before, and by someone he'd wanted to love.

Someone he'd trusted, who had nursed him back to health, who had treated him like a father. He'd learned not to trust anyone, damn it, even the people he loved. Especially the people he loved.

'Do as much damage control as possible,' he instructed Malik. 'I do not want to be fodder for the tabloids. And if people ask, say nothing, give no details. The sooner this is forgotten, the better.'

Malik nodded, his gaze troubled. 'Are you sure…?'

'Yes,' Azim snapped. 'I'm sure.'

Azim didn't return to the banquet, and he didn't send for her that night. Johara went back to her quarters, the hope that had started as a frail and tender shoot in her soul earlier starting to wilt. What had happened? Where had he gone?

She tossed and turned all night, her mind in a ferment of worry and want. Finally, just after breakfast, an attendant summoned her, and Johara's heart lifted.

'Am I going to see Azim, ah, His Highness?' she asked as she followed the man down one of the palace's many corridors. The attendant didn't answer, making the butterflies fluttering in her stomach start to swarm up her throat.

She was let into a small, private room—a study, she realised—and Azim was standing by the window, his back to her. He didn't turn when she entered.

'Azim—'

'You will leave this morning,' he cut her off tonelessly. 'For France.'

Johara gaped. *'France?'*

'Yes. France.' He finally turned with a cold, empty smile. 'Where you wanted to spend most of your time, yes? Now you have your wish. We will have exactly the marriage you wanted to have when we first met.'

'But…' Her head was swimming and she felt dizzy. 'Azim, what has happened? Last night—'

'Last night I learned your true colours. And I realised how foolish I'd almost been again.' He shook his head. 'I will not make the same mistake.'

'What mistake? What's going on?'

He nodded towards his desk. 'That. But of course you already know.'

'That…' It took Johara a moment for her stunned gaze to focus on the paper on the desk—a printout of a newspaper's front page, one of Europe's trashier tabloids. She saw the headline and realisation slammed through her, leaving her breathless. 'You think…you think I have something to do with *that*?'

'You're the only person I told, Johara,' Azim answered coldly. 'The only person ever. So perhaps you should stop playing the aggrieved innocent. I find it rather distasteful.'

'Distasteful?' She drew herself up, fury warring with a deep and terrible pain. She chose fury. 'Do you know what I find distasteful, Azim? That you would think something this horrible of me. That you would make such an awful assumption without even asking me about it. I find that extremely *distasteful.'*

Azim's expression did not soften in the least. His eyes were as hard and dark as they'd been that first day, when he'd told her they would marry. 'Who else could it have been?' he demanded. 'No one else knew, Johara. No one.'

'I don't know,' she admitted. 'But it wasn't me.'

'A flimsy defence,' he scoffed and turned away. 'You can go.'

She stared at his broad back with the now-hidden scars she'd touched and caressed out of love for him. And she'd come so close to believing he might actually love her back—just as she'd once thought her father had loved her.

And just like her father's, Azim's so-called love was cheap and easy. Presents, a garden, sex. Nothing that cost him too much. When it came to the real and demanding price of love—trust and loyalty—he walked away, just as her father had. But this time at least she would have her say.

'Do you know what I think?' she demanded, her voice shaking. She ploughed on without waiting for Azim's dismissive response. 'I think you're a coward.' He turned around, anger sparking in his eyes. 'A big, cowardly *baby*,' she added for emphasis, and his nostrils flared, the skin around his mouth turning white. 'You've been so courageous for most of your life, Azim, and for that I admired you. I loved you. But right now you're being a coward—not about a beating or physical pain, but about the pain you can feel here.' She gestured to her heart. 'I think you know I had nothing to do with that article. How could I? Who did I call, do you think, to spill your story? And why would I do that? What on earth could I gain?'

'Money,' he said tightly, and she let out an incredulous laugh.

'Money? I'm the wife of one of the richest men on the continent. I want for nothing—'

'Your own money. Perhaps you wanted to run away again. Perhaps it was some kind of revenge for being forced to marry me.'

'And what about the last month? What about all the conversations we've had, all the times we've made love? Do you think all of it was an act for me?' She realised tears were streaming down her face and she didn't care. 'Maybe it was for you. Maybe that's what this is about. Or maybe,' she flung at him, swiping at her wet cheeks, 'you got too scared. You were starting to fall in love with me and this provided your convenient excuse to back away and stay safe. Because loving someone is hard, I know. It opens you up to all sorts of pain and grief, because when you love someone they have the power to hurt you. Devastate you.'

She drew a shuddering breath. 'Trust me, I get that. I've felt it. But I'm big enough to take it on. I'm sorry you're not.' A muscle ticced in his jaw but other than that his expression did not change. There was no emotion on his face, not even a flicker of regret or uncertainty. The fury that had been fuelling her sputtered to a stop. 'I'll go,' she said with as much dignity as she could muster. 'I don't want to stay anyway, if you're going to act like this.' With a shaking finger Johara pointed to the printout on the desk. 'But please, for your own dignity as well as mine, don't pretend I had anything to do with that.' Managing to keep her head high with superhuman effort, she stalked out of the room.

The slam of the door ricocheted through Azim's head, adding to the pulsing pain. He'd been fighting a migraine for hours, ever since he'd learned of Johara's betrayal. Her alleged betrayal, but what else could he believe? No one knew the kind of detail that had been in that article. No one but her.

Closing his eyes against a deeper pain than the one in his head, he fought both regret and doubt. What if he'd been wrong? What if he'd sent her away for no reason? Yet this was the kind of marriage they'd planned all along. One of convenience. And if she was in France rather than Alazar, who cared? He'd deal with the issue of an heir later. Maybe, God willing, Johara was pregnant already. That possibility brought another lightning strike of pain. *Johara with his child*...but he couldn't think about that yet. He couldn't think about anything. He'd just known he needed her away from him.

Blindly, the pain too great to ignore or suppress, Azim strode from the room.

Hours later, after a deep, dreamless sleep, the pain had finally receded, even as the pain in his heart increased, overwhelming him. Every pointed and hurt-filled accusation Johara had flung at him played on an endless loop in his mind, filling him with doubt. He wondered if he'd made an enormous mistake—and then wondered if he hadn't. He didn't know what or who to believe, and the last thing he was going to trust was the pointless yearning of his own heart.

A soft tap sounded at the door. 'Azim?'

Azim started to rise, and then fell back against the pillows. Let Malik see him like this. He'd been hiding so much for so long, and now it had all been exposed. What was the point of pretending he didn't get headaches, didn't feel pain?

'Come in.'

Malik came in, frowning when he saw Azim in bed. 'Are you ill—?'

'Migraine,' Azim answered shortly. 'I get them on occasion.'

'I'm sorry.'

He shrugged. 'Is there any news?'

'Yes, we've found the source of the article.' Everything in Azim tensed as he waited for the verdict. 'It's a man named Paolo Caivano.'

'Caivano?' Azim gaped at his brother.

'You know him?'

'Yes, he's…he was the nameless Mafioso of the article. The man who enslaved me.'

'Ah. That makes sense.'

'Does it?'

'I assume he wanted some sort of revenge. When he saw you were the heir to the Sultanate…'

'He thought he could discredit me, and probably got a

decent payment for his tell-all as well.' Azim shook his head. 'I should have guessed.'

'At least now we know. The other tabloids aren't picking it up, and Caivano's been arrested for questioning. Coming up with an article like that wasn't so clever on his part.'

'No.' Azim closed his eyes, realisation washing over him. Johara wasn't guilty. She hadn't betrayed him. And yet he'd tried and convicted her without a single question asked. He was ashamed, but more than that he was afraid. He might have lost the best thing that had ever happened to him, because he knew in that moment she'd been right in every point. He had been afraid…and he did love her.

CHAPTER SIXTEEN

FRANCE WASN'T THE SAME. The home she'd once missed, her beloved garden and stillroom, the friendship of Lucille and Thomas, even her cat Gavroche. None of it made up for the aching absence of Azim. Her husband and the man she loved.

The day after she'd arrived back at the villa Johara sat in the garden, Gavroche on her lap, her heart aching with a heaviness that made her feel weighed down and barely able to move. She'd spent the eight-hour flight from Alazar reliving all the wonderful moments of the last month, and then every agonising second of her final conversation with Azim. How could he have believed that of her? She felt flayed alive by both his accusation and judgment.

'Johara?'

Johara looked up in surprise to see her mother walking towards her. She couldn't remember the last time Naima had been out there.

'Maman...'

Naima smiled tiredly, her face pale as she sat next to Johara on the bench. 'I forgot how lovely it is out here. I should come out more.'

Johara simply stared, hardly knowing how to act with a woman who had absented herself years ago. Naima's smile turned knowing as she met her daughter's gaze. 'I'm sorry,' she said quietly. 'For many things.'

'You...you don't have to be, Maman.'

'But I am.' Naima sighed, the sound soft and sad. 'I have not dealt with life's sorrows as well as I should have.'

'I cannot blame you for that.' Not when she was suffering from her own sorrows.

'Still, I should have paid far more attention to you, and thanked God for the blessing I had rather than the blessing I didn't. It was only that I hoped for so much more from life. From your father especially.'

'I understand.' Johara's throat was thick. As much as she'd wished for her mother's attention and love, she could not begrudge its absence now, not when Naima was actually trying.

'You are very forgiving.' Naima's thoughtful gaze rested on her. 'And now I fear your own marriage might be in trouble.'

'Worse than that.' Johara swallowed hard. 'Azim has sent me away. He believed something terrible of me and now...' She shrugged. 'He wants me to live here.'

Naima's eyes were sad even as she managed a small smile. 'Well,' she said on a sigh, 'it is not such a bad place to live.'

'Were you angry that Father sent you away?' Johara asked. 'All those years ago?'

'Yes, at first. I was heartbroken. I wanted to be by his side, a true and loving wife and partner. But then I had so many miscarriages and each one disappointed your father terribly. I knew he didn't love me, and the losses made it all worse. I broke down, and that was something your father could neither endure nor accept.'

Just like with her, Johara supposed. Her father's 'love' extended only so far. 'I'm sorry, Maman.'

'I'm sorry, too. But perhaps now we can be happy together. Or perhaps your husband will come to his senses.'

'Perhaps,' Johara agreed doubtfully. She'd said a lot of hard words to Azim when she'd last seen him. She didn't know if he could ever forgive her, never mind about that awful newspaper article.

Two days passed with aching slowness. Johara tried to involve herself in her garden, and enjoyed her mother's occasional forays downstairs. They were rebuilding their relationship with painful slowness, but it gave her hope. Hope she sorely needed as the silence from Azim stretched on.

It was high summer and there was plenty to do in the garden, so Johara tried to keep herself busy. She was on her hands and knees, weeding a lavender bed, when she heard footsteps behind her.

'Lucille…?'

'No. Not Lucille.' The achingly familiar voice had her freezing where she knelt, hope warring with disbelief and a remnant of anger. Slowly she turned.

'You have the habit of surprising me in gardens.'

'You have the habit of being in gardens.' The smile Azim gave her was lopsided and wonderful. He looked tired, stubble glinting on his cheeks, his eyes shadowed with uncertainty. Johara sat back on her heels.

'Why are you here?'

'To grovel.'

A smile tugged at her mouth. 'That's a good start.'

'I'm so sorry, Johara. I made a huge mistake. One I can hardly bear to think about now.'

Relief was inflating inside her like a balloon, but still she remained wary. 'And when did you realise this?'

'When my brother told me that it was Caivano who gave the information for the article. He saw my picture in the newspaper and decided to attempt to discredit me, a desperate sort of revenge.'

'Ah.' Johara nodded slowly. 'So you realised you'd been wrong when you had absolute proof, in other words. No trust required.'

He grimaced. 'I admit, I jumped to terrible conclusions. I allowed one betrayal a long time ago to make me expect another.'

'You mean with Caivano.'

'When he rescued me in the hospital, I thought of him as my saviour. I... I loved him, like the father I'd never really had. He took care of me for weeks. He seemed so sincere, and I poured all my confusion and hope into him.' Azim shook his head slowly. 'Even now I wonder why he did it. Simply for free labour? Or was it more sadistic than that, some sort of quest for absolute power over another human being? I don't know.'

'Oh, Azim.' Guilt warred with regret as she took in the import of his words. 'I should have thought about that. I should have realised...'

'No, I should have realised,' Azim insisted starkly. 'You were right about everything. I was afraid.' His voice trembled and Johara knew how hard it was to admit it, and her heart expanded with love. 'Afraid of loving you,' he continued, 'of opening myself up to the kind of pain I gave you. I *am* a coward.' He shook his head in recrimination.

'No, you're not,' Johara said, a fierce note of determination entering her voice. 'I never should have said that.'

'But I'm glad you did, because it woke me up to different kinds of courage.' His eyes blazed as he looked at her. 'And you, my love, are the bravest of them all.'

Johara's heart tumbled in her chest as she took in his words. 'Yes,' Azim said seriously, reaching for her hand and pulling her up from the ground so she was standing in front of him, their hands clasped, sincerity emanating from every taut line of his body. 'I love you. I was fighting it, which was why I stayed away when we returned from the desert. And when the article came out...' He shook his head, regret etched in every line of his face. 'You were right, I did use it as an excuse. A way to justify to myself why I wasn't going to risk anything at all.'

'But I understand why you would have jumped to such conclusions,' Johara protested, 'when virtually the same thing happened to you before.'

'But I knew in my heart that you were different. I've always known you were different, from the moment I met you, and you showed me such spirit. I fell in love with you a little bit that day, Johara, and more and more ever since then.'

Her heart was full to overflowing as he slipped his arms around her waist and drew her closer to him, their hips nudging, her breasts brushing his chest. 'I fell in love with you a bit then, as well,' she admitted.

'Surely not,' Azim returned with a laugh. 'I was most certainly not at my best that day.'

'No,' Johara agreed, 'but you still fascinated me. And when you rescued me in Paris, as terrified as I was of you, I was also incredibly relieved. And thrilled,' she admitted. 'Something in you drew me to you even then.' And then, in case he didn't realise and also simply because she needed to say it, she drew back to look at him seriously. 'I love you, Azim. Never doubt it. I love you with my whole heart and I want a proper, loving marriage with you always.'

'As do I. When we were in the desert I didn't like how you walked behind me—'

'But that's what I was meant to do!' Johara protested.

'Yes, but I didn't like it. I wanted you by my side. I wanted you as my partner.'

She made a face even as a new hope bubbled inside her. 'What about the desert tribes?'

'They'd seen me, met me. And they've seen and met you. I need to live and rule as I believe is right, not to pacify one part of my people.' He brushed a kiss across her lips, his expression soft with love. 'So no more harem.'

'What?'

'You can keep your garden there if you like, or you can have an even bigger garden somewhere else. But you belong with me.'

'By your side or in your bed?' Johara reminded him with a small, teasing smile.

'Yes to both, and Sultana in your own right. I saw how you shone at the banquet, Johara, and everyone in the palace misses you. You've made a lot of fans, you know, in your short time in Alazar. And I'm your biggest one.'

'You're the only one I want, not as a fan, but a friend and lover and husband.'

'I intend to be all three.'

'Good.' She rested her head against his chest, her heart so full of happiness she felt as if she could float right up to the sky. Azim slid his arms around her, drawing her more firmly against him. All was right with the world at last.

'Let's go back to Alazar,' Johara said softly. 'Let's go home.'

* * * * *

MILLS & BOON®
Hardback – May 2017

ROMANCE

The Sheikh's Bought Wife	Sharon Kendrick
The Innocent's Shameful Secret	Sara Craven
The Magnate's Tempestuous Marriage	Miranda Lee
The Forced Bride of Alazar	Kate Hewitt
Bound by the Sultan's Baby	Carol Marinelli
Blackmailed Down the Aisle	Louise Fuller
Di Marcello's Secret Son	Rachael Thomas
The Italian's Vengeful Seduction	Bella Frances
Conveniently Wed to the Greek	Kandy Shepherd
His Shy Cinderella	Kate Hardy
Falling for the Rebel Princess	Ellie Darkins
Claimed by the Wealthy Magnate	Nina Milne
Mummy, Nurse...Duchess?	Kate Hardy
Falling for the Foster Mum	Karin Baine
The Doctor and the Princess	Scarlet Wilson
Miracle for the Neurosurgeon	Lynne Marshall
English Rose for the Sicilian Doc	Annie Claydon
Engaged to the Doctor Sheikh	Meredith Webber
The Marriage Contract	Kat Cantrell
Triplets for the Texan	Janice Maynard

MILLS & BOON®
Large Print – May 2017

ROMANCE

A Deal for the Di Sione Ring	Jennifer Hayward
The Italian's Pregnant Virgin	Maisey Yates
A Dangerous Taste of Passion	Anne Mather
Bought to Carry His Heir	Jane Porter
Married for the Greek's Convenience	Michelle Smart
Bound by His Desert Diamond	Andie Brock
A Child Claimed by Gold	Rachael Thomas
Her New Year Baby Secret	Jessica Gilmore
Slow Dance with the Best Man	Sophie Pembroke
The Prince's Convenient Proposal	Barbara Hannay
The Tycoon's Reluctant Cinderella	Therese Beharrie

HISTORICAL

The Wedding Game	Christine Merrill
Secrets of the Marriage Bed	Ann Lethbridge
Compromising the Duke's Daughter	Mary Brendan
In Bed with the Viking Warrior	Harper St. George
Married to Her Enemy	Jenni Fletcher

MEDICAL

The Nurse's Christmas Gift	Tina Beckett
The Midwife's Pregnancy Miracle	Kate Hardy
Their First Family Christmas	Alison Roberts
The Nightshift Before Christmas	Annie O'Neil
It Started at Christmas...	Janice Lynn
Unwrapped by the Duke	Amy Ruttan

MILLS & BOON®
Hardback – June 2017

ROMANCE

Sold for the Greek's Heir	Lynne Graham
The Prince's Captive Virgin	Maisey Yates
The Secret Sanchez Heir	Cathy Williams
The Prince's Nine-Month Scandal	Caitlin Crews
Her Sinful Secret	Jane Porter
The Drakon Baby Bargain	Tara Pammi
Xenakis's Convenient Bride	Dani Collins
The Greek's Pleasurable Revenge	Andie Brock
Her Pregnancy Bombshell	Liz Fielding
Married for His Secret Heir	Jennifer Faye
Behind the Billionaire's Guarded Heart	Leah Ashton
A Marriage Worth Saving	Therese Beharrie
Healing the Sheikh's Heart	Annie O'Neil
A Life-Saving Reunion	Alison Roberts
The Surgeon's Cinderella	Susan Carlisle
Saved by Doctor Dreamy	Dianne Drake
Pregnant with the Boss's Baby	Sue MacKay
Reunited with His Runaway Doc	Lucy Clark
His Accidental Heir	Joanne Rock
A Texas-Sized Secret	Maureen Child

0517 GEN STD HB

MILLS & BOON®
Large Print – June 2017

ROMANCE

The Last Di Sione Claims His Prize	Maisey Yates
Bought to Wear the Billionaire's Ring	Cathy Williams
The Desert King's Blackmailed Bride	Lynne Graham
Bride by Royal Decree	Caitlin Crews
The Consequence of His Vengeance	Jennie Lucas
The Sheikh's Secret Son	Maggie Cox
Acquired by Her Greek Boss	Chantelle Shaw
The Sheikh's Convenient Princess	Liz Fielding
The Unforgettable Spanish Tycoon	Christy McKellen
The Billionaire of Coral Bay	Nikki Logan
Her First-Date Honeymoon	Katrina Cudmore

HISTORICAL

The Harlot and the Sheikh	Marguerite Kaye
The Duke's Secret Heir	Sarah Mallory
Miss Bradshaw's Bought Betrothal	Virginia Heath
Sold to the Viking Warrior	Michelle Styles
A Marriage of Rogues	Margaret Moore

MEDICAL

White Christmas for the Single Mum	Susanne Hampton
A Royal Baby for Christmas	Scarlet Wilson
Playboy on Her Christmas List	Carol Marinelli
The Army Doc's Baby Bombshell	Sue MacKay
The Doctor's Sleigh Bell Proposal	Susan Carlisle
Christmas with the Single Dad	Louisa Heaton

MILLS & BOON®

Why shop at millsandboon.co.uk?

Each year, thousands of romance readers find their perfect read at millsandboon.co.uk. That's because we're passionate about bringing you the very best romantic fiction. Here are some of the advantages of shopping at www.millsandboon.co.uk:

* **Get new books first**—you'll be able to buy your favourite books one month before they hit the shops

* **Get exclusive discounts**—you'll also be able to buy our specially created monthly collections, with up to 50% off the RRP

* **Find your favourite authors**—latest news, interviews and new releases for all your favourite authors and series on our website, plus ideas for what to try next

* **Join in**—once you've bought your favourite books, don't forget to register with us to rate, review and join in the discussions

Visit **www.millsandboon.co.uk**
for all this and more today!